Flynn watched the tears squeezing out of her closed eyes and, realising he was distressing her further, decided instead to try a different track.

'We'll go through it all later, at the hospital. Let's talk about nicer things. Tell me about yourself, Meg. Come on, Meg. If I'm going to stay with you, the least you can do is talk to me.' His voice was sharp, forcing her out of her slumber. 'Have you got a husband, a boyfriend? Tell me about him.'

'We broke up.'

'Ouch.' He gave a low laugh. 'Trust me to say the wrong thing.'

She opened her eyes a fraction, wincing at the bright morning sun glimpsed through the broken tree. 'He was cheating.'

That was a simple way of putting it, but she was too tired and it was all just too damn complicated to explain.

'Then he's a fool,' Flynn said decisively. 'Forget him.'

A&E DRAMA

Blood pressure is high and pulses are racing in these fast-paced, dramatic stories from Mills & Boon® Medical Romance™. They'll bust a gut to save a life in an emergency, be they a crash team, ER doctors, fire, air and land rescue or paramedics. There are lots of critical engagements amongst the high tensions and emotional passions in these exciting stories of lives and loves at risk!

A&E DRAMA
Hearts are racing!

Carol Marinelli did her nursing training in England and then worked for a number of years in Casualty. A holiday romance while backpacking led to her marriage and emigration to Australia. Eight years and three children later the romance continues... Today she considers both England and Australia her home. The sudden death of her father prompted a reappraisal of her life's goals and inspired her to tackle romance-writing seriously.

EMERGENCY AT BAYSIDE

BY

CAROL MARINELLI

MILLS & BOON®

For Anne and Helen
With love

First published in Great Britain 2003
Harlequin Mills & Boon Limited,
Eton House, 18-24 Paradise Road, Richmond, Surrey TW9 1SR

© Carol Marinelli 2003

ISBN 0 263 17593 6

Set in Times Roman 10½ on 12½ pt.
07-0103-43769

Printed and bound in Great Britain
by Antony Rowe Ltd, Chippenham, Wiltshire

CHAPTER ONE

PULLING off her ID tag and stethoscope, Meg threw them into her locker and, as the changing room was empty, expended some of her frustration by slamming the door shut, then, for good measure, slammed it hard once again.

It didn't help.

She hadn't really expected it too.

'Morning, Meg.' Jess ran in and without pausing for breath started to undress at lightning speed. 'This is the first time in more than thirty years of nursing I've been late. Can you believe it?'

Had it been anyone else Meg wouldn't have believed it, but coming from Jess it was probably true. Trained in the days of starched uniforms and matrons, Jess ruled her world by the little silver fob watch neatly pinned to her crisp white blouse.

'Was that Carla the student nurse I saw leaving here in tears?'

Meg nodded but didn't elaborate—a move she knew would infuriate Jess, who liked to keep her finger on everyone's pulse.

'I thought she was doing really well; at least she has been on days.' Jess's Irish accent was as strong and sharp as Meg's own mother's. Maybe that was the reason Meg's defences seemed to go on high alert whenever Jess approached; she always felt as if she

5

were about to be scolded. 'So, what did you have to tell her off about?' Jess wasn't being nosey—well, maybe a bit—but as they were both Associate Charge Nurses, any problems with the staff had to be discussed.

'I wasn't telling her off.' Meg had pulled on her shorts and T-shirt and was now concentrating on combing the long dark curls, that had been clipped up all night, into some sort of shape before tying her hair loosely into a ponytail. 'She was just upset about a patient we had in last night.'

'Oh, were you busy?'

'No, we were actually quiet for once, which was just as well.' Meg paused before continuing, taking out her scrunchy and combing her hair again before adding, 'We lost a child last night.'

Jess stopped filling her pockets with scissors, forceps and the other paraphernalia that Emergency nurses seemed to magic up at appropriate moments and stood still for a moment. 'How old?'

'Two.' This was where most nurses would have gone into detail. Sat on the bench and told their colleague about the little kid who had been in the bath with no one watching him. The tiny lifeless bundle the paramedics had run in with. The prolonged resuscitation that everyone had known was useless, but no one had wanted to be the one to call. The agony of talking to the parents. The utter desolation at such a senseless waste of a promising young life.

But not Meg.

Meg finished her hair and turned around. 'I'm the peer support person for Emergency so I thought I ought to go over it with her. She's still pretty upset; it was her first death,' Meg added.

'Poor Carla.' Jess took a deep breath. 'Sure, your first death's bad enough when it's a ninety-year-old, but to have a child... Would you like me to have a quiet word with her?' Jess's intentions were well meant, but Meg shook her head.

'She's off for a couple of days—the break will be good for her. But I might get her phone number and give her a ring—see if she wants to catch up for a coffee and go over anything again.'

'What about you, Meg?' Jess's voice was wary; she was unsure of the reaction she might get. 'Do you want to talk about it? I mean, I know you're the peer support person, but that doesn't mean *you* don't need to go over things.' She waited for a response but Meg just stood there. 'If you're upset....'

'I'm fine; this sort of thing comes with the territory. It was hard on Carla because she hadn't witnessed anything like it before; I'm used to it.'

'I know. It's just—' Jess swallowed hard '—this sort of thing affects us all, and if you do need to talk I'm here for you.'

Meg gave a dismissive smile. 'I'm fine, Jess. Honestly.'

To be fair, Jess might be a little irritating, might be a drama queen, but Meg knew she meant well, and had they been sitting in the staff room with a cup of coffee, then maybe she would have opened up a bit. But that was the problem with debriefing, with peer support or trauma counselling, or whatever new name Admin dreamed up for it: sometimes emotions couldn't just be switched on. Jess—busy, rushing to start her shift—together with Meg—weary, teary and ready to go home—wasn't exactly the ideal combination. It just wasn't going to happen this morning.

Jess knew when a conversation was over and decided not to push it, instead choosing sensibly to change the subject. 'Are you staying to meet the new consultant?'

'I'd forgotten about that. Is it this morning he starts, then?'

'Yep, the canteen's even putting on a breakfast in the staff room. Surely you're not going to miss out on a free feed *and* the chance to meet the new boy wonder?'

Meg gave a wry smile. 'He doesn't sound that wonderful to me. From what I've heard, Flynn Kelsey has spent the last two years doing research.'

'Ah, but his research has all been in trauma and resuscitation.' Jess wagged a finger. 'It's all relevant—at least that's the propaganda being fed to us from Admin. The truth is, they're just relieved someone's actually taken up the position; poor old Dr Campbell can hardly run the department alone. Who knows? They might have actually got it right for once and Flynn Kelsey will turn out to be the fantastic doctor that they're promising.'

'If he's that good, what was he doing with his head buried in books for the last two years? Hands-on experience is more relevant,' Meg said firmly. 'We can all sit and read about it. Rolling your sleeves up and getting on with the job does it for me every time.'

'So you're not staying to welcome him?'

'I'm sure I'll meet him soon enough.'

'Come on,' Jess pushed. Meg's red-rimmed eyes were worrying her. 'Just for a quick coffee?'

Meg feigned a yawn. 'Honestly, Jess, I'm exhausted. My bed sounds far more tempting right now.' Picking up her bag, Meg slung it casually over her shoulder. 'Bye then.' As she got to the door Meg paused for a second. 'Oh, Jess, I've left all the paperwork from Luke—the child last night—in the Unit Manager's office. Dr Leighton needs to write up all the drugs that were given; I've left the list clipped to the casualty card.'

'Sure.'

As Meg turned to go she let out a small sigh. 'Poor kid.' Her voice was soft, more a whisper, really, and Jess knew that the words had come out involuntarily. But Meg recovered quickly, smothering her display of emotion with another huge yawn. 'I'm dead on my feet; I'd better get home.'

Meg wasn't tired, not in the slightest. In fact as she drove her small car out of the car park she debated whether or not to stop at the shops and pick up some groceries, knowing that when she got to bed all she was going to do was lie there staring at the ceiling, going over and over the night's events. But shopping was more than she could deal with this morning. Choosing between wholemeal and white, full cream or low-fat milk seemed so trivial, so irrelevant, when a child was dead.

Poor kid.

Driving along Beach Road, for a second Meg hesitated, her foot poised over the brake, wondering whether or not to stop at her parents'. Tea, toast and sympathy from her mother sounded wonderful, but, given the fact that tensions on the home front were running at an all-time high, Meg decided against the idea, instead flicking on her indicator and heading up the hill for home.

Wincing as she changed gear, Meg remembered why her hand was hurting this morning. Remembered Dr Leighton looking over to the flat line on the monitor.

'We've been going for forty-five minutes with no response. I think we should call it. Does anyone have any objections?'

The ampoule of adrenaline Meg had been holding in her hand had shattered then, but she hadn't let on. 'Perhaps we should keep going while I talk to his parents. It might help them to come in and see us still working on him.' Throwing the shattered ampoule into the sharps bin, Meg had wiped her hand and applied a plaster to the small deep cut, then taken a deep steadying breath before heading for the interview room and walking in and delivering the shattering news. The look of utter desolation on Luke's parents' faces as she'd gently broken the news, then walked them the short distance to resus, had stayed with her throughout the night. The utter grief as they had done what no parent should ever have to.

Said goodbye to their child.

Up the winding hill she drove, the stunning view of the bay that filled her car window doing nothing to soothe her. Instead the conversation she had had with Luke's parents replayed in her mind so clearly that it might just as well have been coming from the car's stereo.

Meg had driven this road hundreds, maybe thousands of times. She knew every last bend in it, knew the subtle gear changes that ensured a smooth ride home. But this morning the painful image of Luke and his mother that flashed into her mind, the tears that sprang from her eyes, the sob that escaped from her lips, were all it took to make her lose her concentration. And in that tiny second the bend she had taken so easily, so many times, suddenly loomed towards her. With a start of horror Meg realised she had taken it too fast. Before she could even slam on her brakes the car shot off the road. There was no time to attempt to gain control, no time for any-thing—just a panicked helplessness as she heard someone yelling out, heard the slam of metal, the pop of glass as it shattered around her.

An ear-splitting shriek seemed to be going on for ever. It reminded her of Luke's mother. Only when the car somersaulted and she felt the impact of the wheel thudding into her chest did the screaming stop, and in a moment of clarity before she lost conscious-ness Meg realised that the person who had been screaming was her.

CHAPTER TWO

'IT'S all right Meg. We're going to get you out of there just as soon as we can.' The familiar voice of Ken Holmes, one of the paramedics Meg knew from her time in Emergency, was the first that welcomed her back to the world.

Everything was familiar: the hard collar holding her neck in position, the probe attached to her ear measuring her oxygen saturation. Meg had been out to many motor vehicle accidents with the Mobile Accident Unit and she knew the routine, knew all the equipment that was being used down to the last detail. But the familiarity brought no comfort. None at all.

The morning sun shone painfully into her eyes, and only then did Meg begin to realise the precariousness of her situation. Her car, or what was left of it, was embedded into the trunk of a huge tree. Its ominous creaking, Meg knew, was a sign of its instability. She sat there angled backwards, watching a massive chain slowly tightening around the trunk, and felt a huge jolt as the chain took up the last piece of slack. Every bone in her body seemed to be aching, her tongue felt swollen and sore, and she could taste blood at the back of her throat.

'How much longer until we can free her?' A deep voice from behind her left ear was calling out.

A deep voice that most definitely wasn't familiar.

12

It was the first time Meg had realised someone was actually in the car with her.

'They're still trying to secure the tree. More equipment's on the way.' Ken's voice was calm and even, but Meg could hear the undercurrent of urgency.

'How long?' She heard the edge of impatience in the deep voice and the hesitancy in Ken's before he answered.

'Twenty minutes—half an hour at most.'

'I want to get another IV line into her and check her injuries. Ken, you come and hold her head. I'll get into the front beside her.'

'Do you want to wait for the rest of the equipment before you move?' Again an ominous note was evident in Ken's voice.

'No. Do you?' There was no scorn in the strange voice, no impatience now, and if Meg hadn't quite grasped the danger she was in, hearing Ken being given a choice served to ram home just how vulnerable her situation was.

But Ken didn't miss a beat. 'I'll come in round the other side.'

'Good man.'

Her fuddled mind fought to recognise the masculine voice that was calmly giving out orders as Ken moved into the back and took over holding her head, while her unknown companion climbed over the passenger seat and into what was left of the seat beside her. It took for ever; every tiny movement seemed to ricochet through her body. Unable to move, all Meg could do was listen: listen to his heavy breathing and the occasional curse as a branch or piece of mangled metal halted his progress.

'It's Meg, isn't it?'

She tried to nod, but the hard collar didn't allow for movement. Opening her mouth a fraction, Meg tried to talk. But her mouth simply wouldn't obey her. He seemed to recognise her distress in an instant. 'It's okay. Don't try to talk. My name is Flynn Kelsey. I'm a doctor, and I'm just going to put a needle into your hand so we can give you some more fluids before we move you out.'

He was talking in layman's terms and Meg realised he didn't know that she was a nurse. He probably assumed the paramedics had got her name from her driver's licence or a numberplate check. It was funny how her mind seemed to be focussing on the tiniest, most irrelevant details. Funny how her mind simply wouldn't allow her to take in the horror of her own situation, trapped and helpless in her precariously positioned car.

Through terrified eyes she watched Flynn Kelsey as he set to work. He was a big man, and the small area that had been cut away was fairly restrictive, but he didn't seem bothered by the confined space. The only concession he made was to take off the hard orange hat he was wearing before he set to work quietly. She searched his face, taking in his grey eyes, the high, chiselled cheekbones, the straight black hair neatly cut. Though he was clean shaven, she could see the dusting of new growth on his strong jaw.

Occasionally he would shift out of focus, her immobilised head making it impossible for her to follow him, but through it all Meg felt him beside her. Felt the steadying presence of his touch, the gentle reassurance of his regular breathing. Shifting into view again, for a second his cool grey eyes caught her petrified ones and he gave her a reassuring smile. Only the appearance of another flask of fluid indicated to Meg that the IV bung was already in; a scratch in the back of her hand was small fry compared to the agony everywhere else.

'We're going to be here for a little while yet.'

'Why can't they get me out now?' It was the first time she had spoken and her voice was husky and strained, no more than a whisper, really, and Flynn had to move his head closer to catch her words.

'Once the car's a bit more secure we can get you out.'

Which didn't answer the question. His careful evasion only scared Meg more.

Watching her closely, Flynn registered her deep intake of breath, saw her eyes screw tightly shut.

He recognised her terror.

'You're a lady that likes the truth, huh?' He paused for a moment before continuing, 'Your car came off the road at Elbow's Bend—do you know it?' Meg did know it; she knew it only too well. The sharp bend of road, cut into the rocks, was a favourite lookout point, and, if her memory served her correctly, the only view was that of the bay a hundred metres below. 'Luckily a couple of trees broke your fall, and we're on a nice sturdy ledge which has given us all a bit of room to work.'

She could hear her teeth involuntarily chattering as

Flynn continued talking in quiet calm tones. 'The trees are holding the car and the firefighters have secured us; we're fine for now, but until the rest of the equipment arrives it's probably safer not to try moving you.'

He didn't add just how tenuous her position had been before the emergency services had arrived— didn't casually throw in how both he and Ken had literally put their lives on the line by climbing into the car to be with her.

He didn't have to; Meg had been out to enough accidents to know the score.

'You're going to be okay.'

'Stay,' she croaked, her eyes still screwed tightly shut.

'Oh, I'm not going anywhere; you're stuck with me for a good while yet. Do you know where you are?'

It seemed a silly question, especially given what he had just told her, but Meg knew he was testing her neurological status. 'In my car.' Her voice sounded gravelly, shaky. 'Or what's left of it.'

'That's right.' He squeezed her hand as she started to cry. 'But it's only a car; you're what's important here. Do you remember what happened? Can you remember what caused the accident?' He watched the tears squeezing out of her closed eyes and, realising he was distressing her further, decided instead to try a different tack. 'We'll go through it all later, at the hospital. Let's talk about nicer things. Tell me about yourself, Meg.'

She tried to shake her head, but the collar and Ken held it still. 'I'm tired.'

'Come on, Meg. If I'm going to stay with you, the least you can do is talk to me.' His voice was sharp, forcing her out of her slumber. 'Have you got a husband? A boyfriend? Tell me about him?'

'We broke up.'

'Ouch.' He gave a low laugh. 'Trust me to say the wrong thing.'

Her eyes opened a fraction, wincing at the bright morning sun glimpsed through the broken tree. Golden-brown eyes, he noticed, almost amber in the bright sunlight, thick black eyelashes framing them, glistening with a new batch of tears. She turned her amber headlights to him. 'He was cheating.'

That was a simple way of putting it, but she was too tired and it was all just too damn complicated to explain.

'Then he's a fool.' Flynn said decisively. 'Forget him.'

'That's what I'm working on.'

Flynn laughed. He was shining a pupil torch in her eyes now. 'I meant while you're stuck here. Think of something you really like. I'm not suggesting anything this time; I'd probably just put my foot in it again. What cheers you up?'

She didn't answer; frankly she couldn't be bothered. Closing her eyes, Meg wished he would just go away, leave her alone to rest a while.

'Meg!'

Reluctantly she opened her eyes. 'I'm tired.'

'And I'm bored. Come on, Meg—talk to me. If I've got to sit here with you, the very least you can do is entertain me.'

'The beach.' Running her tongue over her dry bloodstained lips, Meg cleared her throat as best she could. 'I like going to the beach.'

'Do you live near it?'

'Not really.' She was really tired now, her eyelids growing heavy again, the need to sleep overwhelming.

'A bit too expensive, isn't it? Come on, Meg, stay awake. Stay with me here and tell me about the beach.'

'Mum and Dad…'

'Do they live near the beach?'

'On the beach,' she corrected

'And I bet you're round there more often than not?'

She actually managed a small laugh. 'Mum says I use the hotel…' No, that wasn't right. Everything was coming out muddled. Meg forced herself to concentrate. 'I use the house like…' She never finished her sentence, her eyes gently closing as she gave up trying to explain.

'Like a hotel?' The torch was blasting back in her eyes now. 'I bet you do. So, come on, what do when you go to the beach? Body surf? Water ski?' There was a tinge of urgency creeping into his voice. 'Open your eyes and tell me what you do at the beach, Meg!'

The sun was shining brightly when she did, warm and delicious. The same sun that warmed her when she sunbathed, the same birds chirping, the same lazy, hazy feeling as she stretched out on a towel and drifted off. Closing her eyes, feeling its warmth, she could almost hear the ocean, almost imagine she was lying on the soft sand, listening to the children patting sandcastles into shape. The hum of the firefighters' drill was almost a perfect Jet Ski in the distance…

'Meg!' It was him again, breaking into her dream, utterly refusing to leave her be. 'What do you do at the beach?'

'I sleep.'

She heard him half-laugh, half-curse. 'She's practically hypnotised herself here, Ken. Tell them to step on it.'

Whether it was Flynn's insistence or whether the tree was finally secured Meg didn't know, but suddenly the 'jaws of life' were peeling the roof off her car as easily as the foil top on a yoghurt carton. The noise was deafening, the movement terrifying, but through it all Flynn was beside her, holding her hand, soothing her with his presence, until finally a firefighter appeared above them, giving the thumbs-up sign. For the last hour all Meg had wished for was to be free from the mangled wreckage, but now the moment was here suddenly she was scared again.

Bracing herself for movement, she gripped Flynn's hand tighter. 'It's going to hurt.'

'You're going to be fine. Once you're in the ambulance, and I've checked you over, I'll give you something for pain.'

'Promise?'

He gave her a smile. 'Trust me.' He was easing his fingers out of her grip. 'I'm just going around to your other side so I can support your head as they bring you out. I'll speak to you again in the ambulance.'

And with that she had to be content.

He held her head as they skilfully lifted her, taking

charge from the top as they started the slow, painstaking ascent back to the road, relaying his orders in
clear, direct tones, carefully ensuring that her neck
never moved out of alignment, assuming at all times
the worst-case scenario: until an X-ray showed no
fracture of her neck it was safer to assume that she
had one. And though Meg had never been more
scared in her life, never been in more pain, amazingly
she felt safe, knew that she was in good hands—
literally.

Strong hands gently lowered her onto the cool crisp
sheets on the stretcher, and she felt the bumps as they
wheeled her to the awaiting ambulance. Fragments of
the conversations between the police and the firefighters reached her as they jolted along.

'…no skid marks…'

'…the witness said she just veered straight off.'

'…just finished a night shift…'

It was the type of conversation Meg heard nearly
every working day, the tiny pieces of a jigsaw that
would painstakingly be put together, adding up the
chain of events that had led to an accident. Only this
time it was about her.

As they lifted her into the ambulance and secured
the stretcher she ran a tongue over her dry blood-
stained lips.

'Where's Flynn?'

Ken patted her arm. 'He'll be here in a moment.'

'He said he'd be here.' Suddenly it seemed imperative that she see Flynn and tell him what had
happened.

'Just give him a moment, Meg, he's had a rough

morning.' Ken's words made no sense. She was the patient, after all, and the way Ken was talking it sounded as if Flynn was the one who was upset.

'What's she moaning about now?' It was Flynn again, a touch paler and a bit grey-looking, but with the same easy smile and a slight wink as he teased her.

'Are you all right?'

Meg opened her mouth to answer but realised that Ken's question had actually been directed to Flynn.

Flynn muttered something about a 'dodgy pie' and, after accepting a mint from Ken, again shone the beastly pupil torch back into her eyes.

'She's in a lot of pain, Flynn.' Ken was speaking as he checked her blood pressure. 'All her obs are stable. Do you want to head off to the hospital now?'

'I'll just have a quick look first.' Whipping out his stethoscope, he gently moved it across her bruised, tender ribcage. 'Good air entry,' he murmured, more to himself than to anyone else. 'Is it hurting a lot, Meg?'

'I didn't...' Her voice was merely a croak, but it was enough to stop Flynn listening to her chest. Pulling his stethoscope out of his ears, he bent his head forward.

'What was that, Meg?'

'I didn't fall...' But she couldn't finish her sentence. Huge tears were welling in her eyes, sobs preventing her from going further as the emotion of the morning, now she was free from the wreckage, finally hit home.

'It's all right, Meg. Don't try and talk. You're safe

now. I'm going to give you something for the pain.'
His lips were set in a grim line and she could see the
beads of sweat on his forehead, but Flynn's voice was
kind and assured as he continued talking. 'The main
thing is that you're safe.' His grey eyes seemed to be
boring into her, and Meg found that she couldn't tear
her own away. Even as the sirens wailed into life and
the ambulance moved off she found herself still holding his gaze, her eyelids growing heavy as the drug
he had injected took effect and oblivion descended.

'Meg O'Sullivan, we weren't expecting you till tonight. Don't tell me: you just can't stay away from
the place.' Jess chatted away good-humouredly, her
Irish accent thick and strong, as the team lifted her
onto the trolley. There was nothing Emergency staff
dreaded more than being wheeled into their own department, but unfortunately it happened now and then,
and the staff dealt with it with a very special brand
of humour—intimate, yet professional.

'Perhaps she's checking up on you.' Ken Holmes
carried on the joke as they swapped the paramedics'
monitors and equipment for the emergency department's own.

'Or…' Jess smiled as she wrapped a blood pressure
cuff around Meg's bruised arm '…she decided that
she did want to meet the new consultant after all.'

'She works here?' Apart from leading the count as
they'd lifted her over it was the first time Flynn had
spoken since they had arrived in the unit.

'*She* does.' Fifty milligrams of Pethidine on top of
a sleepless night had not only controlled her pain but

also taken away every last piece of Meg's reserve, and her comment came out rather more sarcastically than intended. She saw his perfectly arched eyebrow raise just a fraction as he skilfully palpated her abdomen.

'And what is it you do here, *Meg*?'

'The same as Jess.'

'And what does Jess do?'

God, why all the questions? All she wanted to do was sleep. Closing her eyes, she ignored him, but Flynn hadn't finished yet.

'Meg, what job do you do here?' His voice was sharp, dragging her out of her slumber.

'I'm a nurse,' she answered reluctantly. Maybe now he'd leave her alone.

'What day is it today?'

The interrogation obviously wasn't over. He was testing her reflexes now, lifting her legs slightly and tapping at her knees as he repeated the question. 'Come on, Meg, what day is it today?'

'Pay day.'

Jess laughed. 'It is too. Thank God,' she added. 'My credit card bill is crashing through the roof. Now, come on, Meg—tell the good doctor here what day it is so he can get off to his welcome breakfast.'

'Tuesday.' No, that was yesterday. Meg always got mixed up when she was doing nights. 'Wednesday,' she said, more definitely. 'Today is Wednesday.'

The same small affirmative nod he had used at the accident scene was repeated and Meg gave a relieved sigh.

'Do you remember what happened yet?'

'I had an accident.'

Flynn gave her a thin smile. 'You certainly did. I meant before the accident. Do you remember what caused it?'

She opened her mouth to answer, to tell him exactly what had happened in the hope of finally being allowed to rest, but as she tried to explain Meg felt as if she was trying to recall a dream. Little flashes of the morning would pop into her head, rather like watching a photo develop, but before the picture appeared it would vanish again, and no matter how she fought to remember the images just slipped away.

'Can you remember?' His voice was gentle, as if he realised how much she was struggling.

'No.' The simple word terrified her.

'You will. Just give it time, Meg.'

Turning to Jess, Meg listened as Flynn ordered what seemed an inordinate amount of tests. 'We'll get her over for a C. spine and head CT now, and I want one of her abdomen. She's tender over the spleen. Chest and abdo films, and I want those bloods back from the lab stat, in case she needs a transfusion. It might be better to pop in a catheter.'

'No.' This time the simple word was said much more forcefully, and Flynn and Jess both turned to her simultaneously. 'No,' she repeated. 'I'm not having a catheter.'

'Okay.' Flynn relented. 'But if you haven't passed urine in the next hour I'm getting one put in.' He turned back to Jess. 'Obviously keep her nil by mouth for now. I'd best go and do a quick duty speech, and then I'll be back to check on her. Call me in the meantime if you're in the least concerned.'

He came over to the trolley then and looked down at her, her hair fanning out on the pillow, knotted and full of glass, streaks of blood on her cheeks and her lips bruised and swollen. Yet there was an air of dignity about her, coupled with a wary, but somehow superior look that brought the beginning of a smile to his lips. 'And try not to give her any more Pethidine. I want to do a full neuro assessment when I get back.'

'Are you going?' It was a strange question, one Meg couldn't believe she had just asked.

'Just for a little while, then I'll be back to review you.' That seemed to placate her, and she relaxed back onto the pillow. 'If you're very good Jess and I might even save you a Danish pastry.' He smiled then, properly, for the first time since their eventful meeting.

It was like being rescued all over again.

Closing her eyes, his face still etched in her bruised, muddled mind, Meg let sleep finally wash over and, utterly oblivious to the world, even the hourly neuro obs the staff performed at regular intervals, she slept through what was left of the day.

'She's waking up.'

'Leave her, Kathy. The nurse said not to disturb her.' Mary O'Sullivan's voice had that sharp warning edge that would have sent Meg scuttling straight back to her chair, but it had little or no effect on her sister.

'That was two hours ago. I just want to see she's all right for myself.'

'Do as your mother says, Kathy.' Ted O'Sullivan had as little impact on Kathy as his wife, and as Meg came to it was to the all too familiar strains of her family bickering.

Kathy stood there peering anxiously over her. 'You're awake.' Kathy's eyes filled with tears as she looked down at her big sister.

'No thanks to you,' Mary interjected. 'Can you not obey a simple order, Kathy? The nurse said to leave her be.'

'Hello, Mum,' Meg croaked. 'Sorry for all the trouble.'

'No trouble—apart from a coronary when the police came to the door.' Mary's attempt at a joke felt more like a telling off, and Meg closed her eyes again, the bright lights of the Emergency observation ward too much for her fragile head. 'Are you all right, pet?'

Keeping her eyes closed, Meg nodded. Now the collar was off at least she was able to do that. It was about the only thing she could do; her chest felt as if a bus was sitting on it. Mary fussed and chatted for a while, but Meg could almost sense her relief when six o'clock came and her mother had a valid reason to go home.

'That lovely Irish nurse, Jess, has kept us up to date. She's away home now, to her husband, but she said that you were to rest as much as possible. Now that you've come to, I might get your father home for his dinner. His insulin was due half an hour ago. I'll be back in first thing tomorrow and we'll ring the ward tonight.'

Again Meg sensed the sting of disapproval.

'Are you coming, Kathy?'

'No.' Meg felt the bed move as Kathy perched herself on it. 'I'll stay with her. Jake can always give me a lift later.'

'She was only joking about the police,' Kathy said when their parents had finally gone.

'Since when did Mum joke?'

'There's always a first time. I was in the hydro pool and Jess let Jake know. It was Jake that went and told her.'

Meg looked at her sister. Her uncombed, spiky blonde hair and the faint scent of chlorine certainly held up her story. 'So the police didn't come?'

'No.' Kathy laughed, but her brimming eyes belied her casual chatter. 'Actually, you did me a favour. They've got a new chief of physio and the workout they were putting me through felt like an army training camp—and, despite what she says, Mum's had a grand afternoon gossiping to Jess about the fair Emerald Isle.'

Meg attempted to smile, but it died on her lips.

'She was upset, you know.' Kathy squeezed Meg's hand. 'Really upset.'

'And now she's angry.'

'You know what Mum can be like.'

Meg did know—only too well. The last few months had been a nightmare. It was bad enough finding out that your boyfriend of eighteen months, the man you'd adored, actually thought you had a future with, was in fact married. And not just married. Married to your colleague's sister, who just happened to go to the same church as your mum. So not only had Meg felt the wrath of disapproval from her colleagues at Melbourne City Hospital, there had been the wrath of her mother to deal with.

Mary O'Sullivan wasn't sure which was the greater of the two evils. The fact her eldest daughter had been branded a home-wrecker, or the undeniable fact that Meg wasn't a virgin.

And now she had trashed her car.

'I hate this year.'

'I know, but there's always next year.'

'Next year will probably be just the same.'

'It won't.' Kathy insisted. 'You've got a new job, new friends, a whole new start. All you have to do is loosen up a bit.'

'Loosen up?'

'Try letting people in. It's a nice world out there. I know Vince hurt you, but not all men are the same.'

Just the mention of his name bought forth a whole fresh batch of tears. Meg hadn't cried since the day they broke up, and certainly not in front of anyone, but the egg on her head combined with the pain in her chest was such a horrible combination that for once crying came naturally.

'I've got some news that might cheer you up,' Kathy said desperately. Seeing her sister, who never cried, sobbing in the bed was torture. 'How do you fancy being a bridesmaid?'

Like a tap being turned off, Meg instantly stopped crying, her eyes swinging round to her sister.

'You're engaged?'

'I have been for…' Kathy glanced at her watch. 'Twenty hours now. He asked me last night.'

'Who, Jake?'

Kathy gave a gurgle of laughter. 'No, the tram conductor. Of course it's Jake. Who else?'

'What does Mum have to say about it?' Meg asked slowly.

'Well, the fact we want to get married so quickly— on Valentine's Day, actually—led to a few sticky questions, but we've finally managed to convince her that it's not a shotgun wedding. We're just head over heels and want to do it as soon as possible. She's tickled pink, actually, and insisting that we have an engagement party. But I've told her that the most we want is a casual dinner.'

Meg gave a wry laugh. 'So no doubt she'll spend tomorrow on the telephone, ringing up hundreds of relatives.'

'Probably,' Kathy conceded. 'But after she's been in to see you, of course,' she added hastily. 'Whoops, look like I'd better make myself scarce—here comes Flynn now.'

Meg screwed up her forehead. 'Flynn? Do you know him?'

'He's a friend of Jake's...' As Flynn approached the bed Kathy's voice trailed off.

'Good evening, Meg—Kathy.' He gave her sister a friendly nod.

'Hi, Flynn. I'll leave you to it; see you in the morning, Sis.' Popping a quick kiss on Meg's cheek, Kathy limped off.

'How are you feeling?'

'Better. Well, sore but better.' The beginning of a blush was creeping over her cheeks.

'That's good. You've had a very lucky escape, Meg, all your tests have come back as normal. Apart from a lot of bruising, which is going to hurt for a while, and a mild concussion, you've got off very lightly.' He peered at his notes for a moment, and Meg watched as he fiddled uncomfortably with his pen. 'Can you remember what happened yet?'

Meg shook her head. Normally she would have left it there, but there was something about Flynn, something about the way he had smiled at her this morning, the drama they had shared, that made her take the plunge and for the first time in ages prolong a conversation. 'No, but I do remember you offering to save me a Danish pastry. You didn't, by any chance, did you?'

Her attempt at small talk was instantly to her dying shame rebuffed.

'Apparently the police seem to think that you might have fallen asleep at the wheel.'

Embarrassed at his businesslike tone, Meg felt her blush only deepen. 'I didn't!'

'There were no skid marks at the scene, and apparently you were exhausted when you left this morning—though Jess told only me that, I hasten to add. I haven't written it in my notes.' He ran a hand through his hair, an exasperated tone creeping into his voice. 'Why the hell didn't you get a taxi?'

She knew he was wrong, knew somehow that the picture he was painting wasn't how it had happened, but her total lack of recall didn't put her in the best position to argue the point.

'I didn't fall asleep,' Meg intoned.

'The police…'

'The police are wrong,' she retorted quickly. 'And anyway, it's none of your business.' She knew she was being rude, but something about Flynn had her acting completely out of character. The little hint about the Danish pastry, the blush that wouldn't go away—and now she was answering him back. It wasn't actually out of character. It was more the old Meg. The Meg before Vince had extinguished every last piece of her fiery personality.

Flynn begged to differ. 'Oh, but it is my business, young lady. It became my business at precisely four minutes past eight this morning, when I stabilised your neck in the wreckage of your car.' His voice was curt and formal, with no hint of the man who had held her hand just this morning, cajoled her to stay awake—who, even in the most dire of circumstances, had actually managed to make her laugh. 'It became my business when I found out that one of the nurses in my department was so damned tired after her night shift she nearly killed herself. And,' he added, standing over her so she had no choice but to look at him, 'had you wiped out an entire family, no doubt it would have been left to me to deal with it. So you see, *Meg*—' his lip curled around her name '—it is my business.'

Despite his anger, it wasn't a no holds barred attack, Meg realised. Not once had he mentioned the very real danger he had put himself in by staying with her throughout the ordeal, and his modest omission somehow touched her.

He stood there for a moment, his eyes challenging

her to respond, but she was too tired and too utterly defeated to argue. 'Right, then. I've spoken to your parents, and I'm happy for you to be discharged tomorrow as long as you go and stay with them.'

'That's all I need,' Meg muttered ungraciously.

'I want the physio to see you before you go and run through some deep breathing exercises. Your chest is badly bruised and it's important he sees you.'

'No.'

Flynn let out an exasperated sigh.

'The catheter I can understand your objection to— but physio, for heaven's sake? Do you have to argue about everything?'

'You don't understand.'

'So enlighten me.'

'Jake Reece is the Emergency physio,' Meg started, her eyes darting around the obs ward to check that Kathy had definitely gone.

'So why is that a problem?

'He's marrying my sister.'

Flynn's face broke into a grin then, and for a second he looked like the Flynn from this morning. 'Jake and Kathy are getting married? That's fantastic news.' He seemed to remember she was there then, and stared at her, perplexed. 'So why on earth don't you want him to see you?'

'Because, unlike you, I'm not exactly thrilled with the news.'

'Why?' He seemed genuinely bemused and Meg couldn't believe that he didn't understand how she was feeling.

'He's her physiotherapist, for heaven's sake. Kathy's handicapped. It's wrong.'

His face changed. She saw his bemused look change to one of distaste.

'Please don't try to tell me that you're so politically correct you haven't even noticed.'

'Of course I've noticed. Kathy has also told me about it herself. Unlike you, she doesn't seem to have a problem with it. From what I can remember of our conversation, she has mild cerebral palsy from birth, which has left her with a limp and a minor speech impediment. What she didn't tell me, but I soon found out for myself, is that she happens to be a fun, happy, caring and very attractive woman.'

'He's ten years older than her.'

'Hardly a hanging offence.' He paused then, eyeing her carefully before continuing. 'As you yourself pointed out, he's her physio, not her doctor. They will have spent a lot of time together. If you got down off your high horse and actually spent some time with them, instead of judging them, you might find yourself pleasantly surprised.'

And, after signing off her discharge papers, he left her lying there.

Lying there for all the world wishing the ground would open up and swallow her.

CHAPTER THREE

MEG's childhood had ended at nine years old.

The day Kathy was born.

She had spent endless afternoons sitting after school in a waiting room doing her homework while Mary took her youngest daughter to a seemingly never-ending round of appointments. Paediatricians, speech therapists, occupational therapists—the list had been endless.

The only person who had taken it all in her stride, literally, had been Kathy. Defying the doctors' grim prognosis, she had cheerfully picked herself up, over and over, until finally at the age of four she had taken her first steps. Her optimistic, sunny nature had served her well in the playground also, with Kathy making friends easily and keeping them. A group of little girls Meg had referred to as 'Kathy's army'. But Kathy's army hadn't always been there for her, and the playground hadn't been the only place a child like Kathy could run into trouble or become the victim of a cruel and thoughtless taunt.

So, from the day Kathy had come home from the hospital, Meg had taken it upon herself to look out for her. It was almost as if Meg had been fitted with an inbuilt radar, constantly on the alert, always looking out for her little sister.

And even though the callipers had long since gone,

even though Kathy was nineteen years old now, and, as Flynn had pointed out, extremely attractive with a social life that would exhaust anyone, Meg's radar was still there. The protective feelings Meg had for her little sister hadn't faded one iota. That was why she was cautious of Jake. She certainly wasn't the bigot Flynn had implied. Her concern here was only to save Kathy from being hurt. After all, Meg knew better than most how easily your heart could be broken.

But a couple of weeks at home, hiding away in her old bedroom, reading again the wonderful books that had fuelled her childhood and eating the inordinate meals that appeared every few hours, had given Meg plenty of time for reflection and introspection, and somewhere along the way Meg had finally realised that Kathy neither wanted nor needed saving.

But Kathy wasn't all that Meg had dwelled on as her sick leave days ticked by into double figures. Hesitantly, painfully, Meg had travelled the bitter-sweet journey of the brokenhearted. Bitter because, bruised and battered, and with a good excuse to cry, Meg had allowed herself to finally grieve—grieve for the man she had lost, the man she had thought Vince was. And sweet because, despite the pain, despite the soul-searching as her blackened chest turned to a dirty yellow and her swollen lips finally went down, for the first time in six months Meg actually knew she was finally over him.

'I've brought you some soup.'

Meg screwed up her nose as Kathy peered around

the bedroom door, a laden tray in her hands. 'I'm sick of soup.'

'How do you think I feel? I wasn't even in an accident and I'm having lentil broth forced down me twice a day. At least you can afford to put some weight on; I'm going to be huge for my party at this rate.'

'What happened to the "casual dinner"?'

Kathy laughed. 'Mum got involved, that's what happened. How she's managed to book a hall and caterers at such short notice I've no idea. I shudder to think what the wedding's going to be like. Half of me just wants to get a licence and get it over and done with, without all the fuss.'

Raining salt on her soup, Meg didn't look up. 'And the other half?'

'The other half of me is starting to buy all the bridal magazines and is wrestling between crushed silk and organza, and lilies as opposed to freesias. I guess the upshot is I can't wait to be married.'

This time Meg did look up. Seeing her sister sitting on the edge of her bed, her face glowing, her eyes literally sparkling, Meg knew she had never seen Kathy looking happier. 'You really love him, don't you?'

'I really do.' Kathy paused for a moment. 'And the best bit of it all is that I know Jake loves me—all of me—even down to my limp. He says that if it wasn't for my limp we'd never have met, which is a pretty nice way of looking at it.'

It *was* nice, Meg admitted to herself. Actually, in the last few days she had found herself looking at

Jake rather differently. He had treated Meg with professional friendliness at the hospital, and as—thanks to Flynn Kelsey—she had been forced into spending the last two weeks at home, there had been plenty of time to watch Jake and Kathy together. Jake even took Mary's somewhat overbearing nature in his stride.

'How do you feel about going back to work tomorrow?'

Meg shrugged. 'It will be nice to get away from the soup.'

'I wouldn't bet on it. Mum's just bought a massive stainless steel vacuum flask; you'll be supping on her Irish broth for weeks yet.' When Meg didn't laugh Kathy continued tentatively. 'A bit nervous, huh?'

Meg nodded. 'A bit,' she admitted. 'It doesn't help that everyone thinks I fell asleep at the wheel.'

'It will be old news soon. They'll soon find something else to talk about.'

'I just wish I could remember what happened.'

'You will.'

Meg fiddled with her spoon. 'I feel as if I've been away for months, not just a couple of weeks. I'm more nervous than when I first started there.'

'Once you've been there a couple of hours you'll soon be back in the swing of things. They seem a nice bunch of girls; you should try to get to know them better. That Jess was lovely to us while you were sleeping.'

'Oh, Jess is nice. She can be a bit overbearing, but it's all well meant. She's probably the one I'm closest to, but a night out with Jess isn't going to do my social life wonders—it would be like going out with Mum.'

'What about the rest of them?' Kathy asked.

'They all seem nice enough,' Meg replied. 'But I don't really know them. I mean, we chat about work and what we did on our days off, but apart from Jess I don't really know much about any of them.'

'And whose fault is that?' Kathy said gently. 'Look, Meg, I know you've had it tough recently, but it's really time to move on, let the world in a bit.'

Meg nodded. 'I know it is.'

Kathy put a hand up to her sister's forehead, an incredulous look on her face. 'Quick—call a doctor! The girl must be delirious. You're not actually agreeing with me, are you?'

Meg grinned as she pushed Kathy's hand away. 'For once I am. Bloody Vince.'

'Absolutely,' Kathy agreed, grinning broadly. 'That's more like it. There's a whole world out there full of gorgeous *single* men.'

'Hold on a moment,' Meg said quickly. 'A relationship's the last thing I want at the moment. I'm talking about resuming a social life, nothing else. I mean it,' she added as Kathy gave her a questioning look.

'I believe you,' Kathy said, but just as Meg started to relax a meddling look flashed across her sister's face. 'But if there was anyone you wanted me to add to the party list, you know you'd only have to ask?'

For a nanosecond Meg's mind involuntarily flashed to Flynn—the Flynn who had sat with her in the car, not the jackbooted doctor who had visited her in the obs ward—but resolutely she pushed all thought of him away. That was one path she definitely wasn't heading down—and anyway, the last person she wanted to help with her love life was her little sister; a girl had to have some pride! 'I'm quite capable of sorting out my own social life, thank you very much.'

Kathy grinned, not in the slightest bit bothered by Meg's haughty tones. 'Okay, okay, it was only a suggestion.' Picking up the last of Meg's bread, she popped it into her mouth. 'At least it's a start.'

A small start, perhaps, but to Meg it felt monumental. This time when she pulled on her uniform and clipped on her badges she forced a smile as she made her way out to the department, utterly determined that when someone suggested heading off to the bar after work, or a house party next weekend, instead of murmuring her usual excuses she would smile warmly and agree to go.

'Morning, Meg, welcome back.'

'Good morning, Carla, how are you?'

Unless it was Carla.

Meg quickly made a sub-clause in her self-imposed contract. A students' bash with cheap wine and even cheaper comments from the medical and nursing students she could do without. She wasn't that desperate.

Yet.

'Fine.' Carla flicked her long blonde fringe out of her eyes and Meg watched as it promptly fell back over them, tempted to tell her to take a bandage from the trolley and tie the shaggy mess back. But, in the spirit of it being her first day back, Meg said nothing. Jess could sort Carla out later.

'Where are you working this morning?'

'I'm in the cubicles at the moment, but Jess said that if anything comes into resus I'm to go in.'

Meg heard the nervous note in the young student's voice. 'You'll be fine. No one will expect you to do anything, you're just there to observe, and when you're feeling up to it you can join in.'

'Thanks. Will you be in there?'

Meg was saved from answering as Jess appeared, crisp and fresh in her white linen blouse. 'How about it, Meg? Do you fancy starting back in the deep end? We're a bit low on numbers this morning, and I'm supposed to be going to an occupational health and safety lecture at ten. I can't believe it's been two years since my last.'

'No problem,' Meg answered, before turning to give Carla a reassuring smile. 'Dr Campbell is really nice to work with in resus.'

'Except he's on two weeks' annual leave.' Jess rolled her eyes. 'Flynn's on this morning. If it's quiet he wants to lecture the students and the grad nurses in CPR—or BLS, as it's called now. Why do they have to keep changing things? And when does this place ever stay quiet?' she asked, but as usual didn't bother to wait for an answer. 'I've told him Annie is off having her arm stitched back on, but he still wants to go ahead.'

'What happened to Annie?' Meg asked. Annie, the plastic doll the staff practised their lifesaving skills on, was a popular member of the staff, and the concern in Meg's voice was genuine.

'My lips are sealed,' Jess said dramatically, which meant she was pausing for breath before she continued. 'Let's just hope that next time our dear Dr Kelsey tries to show the new interns how to reduce a dislocated shoulder, he'll leave poor Annie alone. The man doesn't know his own strength.' Tutting away, Jess turned her attention to Carla. 'In my day—and, I hasten to add it wasn't *that* long ago—we wore hats, and with good reason. Now, go and do something about that blessed fringe of yours or I'll make you wear a theatre cap for the rest of your rotation.'

As she bustled off Carla rolled her eyes and turned to Meg. 'She talks as if she trained during the Second World War; just how old is Jess?'

'Fifty-something,' Meg mumbled.

'Oh, well, I guess that explains it,' Carla replied, accepting the bandage Meg offered her and managing to still look gorgeous with a massive white bow on the top of her head.

'Which means she's got a lot of experience,' Meg said pointedly, annoyed at Carla's surly comments. 'I know first-hand what a good nurse she is—and not just from a professional point of view. Jess is the first person you want to see when you're coming through those doors on a stretcher. Tying up your hair and looking smart might seem minor details, but they're important ones; it goes a long way to instilling confidence in the patients.' Suitably chastised, Carla followed Meg into resus.

'I know it seems *boring* how we constantly check

all the equipment, but it really is vital,' Meg explained as she painstakingly checked and restocked all the backboards behind the resus bed. 'Everything has its own place in s resuscitation room. There isn't time to be rummaging through shelves when someone is desperately ill and staff are already tense. It's much easier all round if everything is well stocked and in order.'

'I couldn't agree more.'

Meg didn't need to look up to know who the deep voice that filled the room belonged to. But in the spirit of her new-found openness she forced a smile as she battled with a blush, painfully aware that the last time they had been together in this room she had been dressed only in a skimpy hospital gown with a good dose of Pethidine on board. Not the best of looks!

'Morning, Flynn,' Carla announced cheerfully, and Meg frowned at the rather too familiar tone.

'Morning, Carla.' Flynn did a double take. 'Have you got a toothache or something?'

'Nah.' Carla shrugged. 'Apparently my hair was a health hazard.'

'Good morning, *Dr Kelsey*,' Meg responded, casting a pointed look at Carla, but Flynn didn't seem remotely fazed by the student's familiarity.

'Flynn will do. Dr Kelsey's my father.'

Meg realised she was gnashing her teeth; between the two of them they had managed to make her feel as if she was about to start drawing her pension. 'Well, in that case,' she said in a rather falsely cheerful voice, 'good morning, Flynn.'

At least she wasn't the only one blushing, Meg

realised—Carla was positively beetroot. But then who could blame her? Students had hormones too, and Flynn was a pretty impressive sight for seven-thirty in the morning. Everything about him oozed masculinity—not just his huge, powerful build, but also the husky voice, the spicy tang of cologne, even the hint of legendary strength, added a touch of zest to an otherwise routine morning.

'You're looking better than the last time I saw you. How are you feeling?'

'I'm fine, thank you.'

But Flynn didn't look convinced. 'I wasn't expecting to see you back so soon. That was a nasty accident you were involved in.'

'Which I'm over.' Meg bristled, unnerved by his scrutiny.

'Hey, I'm just the doctor.' Flynn grinned. 'Still, if it does turn out too soon for you to be back just let me know and I'll sign you off.'

'Wouldn't you just?' Meg muttered, but Flynn wasn't listening. Instead he was looking around the room, pulling from the walls half the equipment Meg had only just replaced.

'What are you doing?'

'Setting up for my lecture. Where's Annie?'

'But I haven't finished checking resus,' Meg argued. 'And Jess said she'd already told you that Annie was off being repaired. Someone,' Meg said accusingly, 'apparently used her as a sparring partner.'

'I did not,' Flynn said defensively. 'I was trying to show the interns how to reduce a shoulder.' He flashed a smile and Meg knew there and then that he'd get his lecture. 'Hey, Carla, any chance of rustling me up a coffee and then grabbing the other students? I'd like to get started.'

Only when Carla had willingly dashed off did Flynn speak again. 'Before you tell me off, I don't usually use the students as tea girls, but I wanted to get you alone and apologise.'

Meg was caught completely unawares, and in an attempt to cover up her embarrassment at suddenly finding herself alone with him her words came out far sharper than intended. 'For wrongly accusing me of falling asleep at the wheel or insinuating that I'm a bigot?'

But Flynn just laughed. 'Feisty, aren't you? And to think I thought it was the Pethidine!'

Meg sucked in her breath. Damn this man, he really managed to get under her skin. 'I thought this was supposed to be an apology?'

'So it is.'

She waited, not quite tapping her foot, but her stance showed her impatience.

'About Kathy,' he started. 'Look, I just went off at the deep end. I was more riled at you falling asleep at the wheel.' He saw her open her mouth to argue and put his hands up. 'Or ''allegedly'' falling asleep. I took Jake and Kathy out for a celebratory drink the other night and had my ear bent about what a wonderful sister you are. I won't embarrass you by going into detail, but the upshot is I know now that I was way out of order.'

He didn't look particularly sorry. 'Is that it?'

Flynn shot her a surprised look. 'Do you want it written in blood? Tell you what, how about I take you out for a drink or dinner? Show that there's no hard feelings?'

Sub-clause B, Meg thought quickly as she shook her head. 'That won't be necessary, thank you.' Delicious consultants with an over-supply of confidence and sex appeal were a definite no-no.

'Oh, come on,' Flynn said easily. 'It would save us both a heap of trouble—I've got a feeling your sister's in a matchmaking mood. Maybe we should just get it over with, before she deafens us both singing the other one's praises.'

'Are you always so romantic when you ask a woman out, Doctor? Because if the way you've just asked me is an indication of your usual approach, it's no wonder you need my sister to help you.'

Flynn just roared laughing. 'Is that a no, then?' he asked as the students started trickling in.

'Yes,' Meg muttered blushing to her toes. 'I mean, yes, it's a no.'

'Pity,' Flynn murmured, and with an easy smile turned his attention to the gathered crowd.

Meg had to hand it to him. Within seconds of starting he had the students and nurses enthralled. BLS, or basic life support, was a subject they would all have covered at college, and on their ward rotations, but here in Emergency, given that it was an almost daily event, they would practically be guaranteed a chance to witness and, if at all possible, practise the life-saving skill.

And Flynn held them in the palm of his hand, explaining that what they learnt today and in their weeks in Emergency might never be needed in their entire career, depending upon their chosen field. 'But...' He paused, those expressive grey eyes working the room, ensuring he had everyone's attention. 'Statistically speaking—and I'm not talking about while you're at work; I'm talking about when you're at the library or doing the groceries, or dropping a video off at the shop—somewhere in the future, someone in this room will utilise this skill, possibly on a stranger, but maybe on someone you love. And you, as nurses, have a chance of doing it right; have a chance of saving a life. Pretty exciting, huh?'

He grinned at the rapt faces. 'So how about a practice?'

'We can't. Annie's still being repaired.' Meg pointed out again.

'Good.' Flynn grinned. 'Then we'll practise on a human—far more realistic than a doll, don't you think? Come on, Meg.'

She hesitated—and for more than a brief moment. Had it been Dr Campbell or Jess—anyone, in fact— Meg would have leapt up on the trolley without a second thought. After all, in her six months here she had been strapped to the ECG machine, been plastered, even had blood taken all in the name of practice. It was part and parcel of the job. But it wasn't Dr Campbell asking her, it was Flynn Kelsey, and lying on the trolley pretending to be a mannequin... Well, suffice it to say there was nothing remotely mannequin-like about the butterflies flying around in her stomach.

'Come on, Meg,' Flynn said impatiently. 'Unless you need a refresher course as well?'

Reminding herself she did this sort of thing all the time, Meg climbed on the trolley and lay back against the pillow, wishing her beastly blush would fade.

'Now, this patient looks well, as you can see. Her colour's excellent—quite pink, actually.' Meg was tempted to take a swipe at him as their audience started laughing. 'But don't be fooled. High colour in an unresponsive patient could be an indication of any number of things. Any ideas?'

'Carbon monoxide poisoning?' Carla said, and Meg made a mental note to praise her later.

'Excellent,' Flynn said warmly. 'Flats with old heaters, suicide attempts, house fires—all these can cause carbon monoxide poising. The patient might look pink and healthy but in reality they're exactly the opposite. Okay, so we've dragged this poor woman out of her flat, she's as red as a beetroot and completely unresponsive—so what now?'

'Check her airway,' a couple of the students called out.

'Good start.' She could feel his fingers on her jaw—firm, warm fingers, Meg noted, squeezing her eyes closed and desperately attempting to relax her face as he gently pulled her chin down. 'Yep, airway's clear. If it wasn't, here in resus obviously I'd use suction. Out on the street it would be with more basic means.' He held up a finger and the students groaned. 'Now what?'

'Check her pulse.'

'She can have the strongest pulse in medical history,' Flynn replied quickly, 'but if she's not breathing what is her heart pumping? Certainly not oxygenated blood. Come on, guys—ABC, remember? We're heading into danger time here; this long without oxygen and you're starting to look at brain damage. Okay—A for airway, B for breathing. Watch her chest to see if it's moving.'

Meg felt ten pairs of eyes on her chest and wondered if he expected her to hold her breath to make things more realistic. A distinct impossibility as suddenly her breath was coming out in short, rapid bursts.

'So, she's not breathing and I'm feeling for a pulse—which…' Meg heard the tiniest hint of a laugh in his voice as he placed his fingers on her neck and felt her fast, flickering pulse '…is absent. Right, because she's an adult I'm going to tilt her neck to open the airway; on an infant you wouldn't do this,' he added, sliding a hand under her neck and jerking her head backwards. 'Babies' necks are shorter and straighter. In an adult pinch the nostrils, so all the air you breathe in doesn't escape. Again it's different for a baby. In that instance you would place your mouth over both the nose and mouth. Anyway—' he coughed slightly '—this isn't a child, this is a full-grown woman. So we tilt the neck, pinch the nostrils and give two effective inflations.'

She could feel his fingers around her nose, gently pinching her nostrils together. One hand was pulling her mouth open and Meg realised with alarm she could feel him moving closer, feel his hot breath on her cheeks. Opening her eyes in alarm, Meg found herself looking into the deep pools of his. Surely he wasn't going to actually do it? This was a practice, for heaven's sake!

But before she could react, register a protest, even if she had wanted to, he had moved his face and given two fast breaths into mid-air, just as any professional would. But there was nothing, *nothing* very professional about the sudden sharp shift in tempo, the crackling awareness that made every touch, every tiny movement send a massive voltage of charged energy tearing through her body. He might just as well have grabbed the defibrillator beside him and charged it to two hundred joules.

'Right.' His voice was perfectly normal. 'Now we can get some of that oxygenated blood pumping through her system. Feel for the bottom half of the sternum and place the heel of your hand on the chest. Very importantly, remember your own strength. By now you'll be pumping with adrenaline yourself, and you don't want to crack the ribcage before you've started.' Mercifully, he removed his hands, then turned to his audience. 'Obviously you never practise massage on a person, so we'll have to wait for Annie to fully recuperate before you all have a turn. But if there's a cardiac arrest in progress in resus and you feel up to it ask one of the trained staff if you can have a go. Nothing beats first-hand experience.'

The BLS demonstration might have been finished, but Meg's questionable hell wasn't over yet. The lecture went on for ages, with the students learning—courtesy of Meg's neck—the finer points of crico-thyroid pressure to assist the doctor during intubation. Her limbs were also subjected to the clumsy students' attempts to place her in the recovery position. All in all, by the time Flynn had finished, and Meg was wearing a blood pressure cuff and possibly the same hard collar she had worn for her accident, despite all her earlier good intentions she wasn't in the best of moods.

'Can I get up now?' she asked rather indignantly when the students rapidly dispersed for their fifteen-minute tea break.

Flynn roared with laughter. 'I'd better give you a hand.' Looking down at her, he grinned. 'A certain *déjà vu*, don't you think?'

'I'd rather not be reminded, thank you.' Taking his offered hand, she let him sit her up, then ripped the blood pressure cuff off as Flynn undid the neck collar. 'Hold still. Some of your hair has got stuck in the Velcro. Here, hold your hair up.' He took her hand and guided it to the pile of curls he had unceremoniously dumped on her head.

'Ow,' Meg squealed as he ripped open the fastening and took half her hairline with it in the process.

'Sorry,' Flynn muttered, but he didn't sound it in the slightest. 'Sorry,' he said again, but this time with more conviction.

Her acceptance died on her lips as she looked up into his eyes. The humour and arrogance had gone; instead his eyes were suddenly serious, and the personal space he had so haplessly invaded suddenly felt inviting and strangely familiar. For Meg there was no question of not moving towards him, no thought of anything other than their lips meeting, a tender yet definite need that pulled them closer.

It was, quite simply, a kiss that had to be.

'Just as I thought,' he murmured, gently pulling away. 'Most kissable.'

'You shouldn't have done that.' Confused, embarrassed, Meg stood up.

'I didn't sense much resistance.' The same easy smile was back, and Meg was sure he was laughing at her, positive that he had kissed her just because he could. Just because she had let him.

'It was an accident,' Meg retorted, furious with him, but more so with herself for succumbing so easily.

Flynn laughed. 'We're in the right room for it, then.'

An uncomfortable silence followed—at least it was for Meg; Flynn didn't seem remotely bothered and made no effort to break it. He was probably, Meg thought angrily, used to necking with willing nurses at inappropriate moments. Used to endless reams of willing woman prepared to jump for his attention, happy to share him around so long as they had their moment in the sun with him.

Well, gorgeous he might be, and sexy and irresistible too, Meg thought reluctantly, but if Flynn thought he was going to use her to boost his already inflated ego then he had another think coming. He might have got away with a quick kiss when she wasn't paying attention, but she wasn't going to let down her guard again.

No way.

From somewhere outside a car was sounding its horn, loud enough to drag Meg back to reality, and she set about clearing away the inordinate amount of equipment Flynn had used for his demonstration, determined not to let him see how his teasing kiss had affected her.

'Meg, look, maybe we should...' The car horn broke into whatever he was about to say and Meg realised that she was frowning.

Flynn noticed it too. 'Something wrong?'

'I don't know.'

Cars tooted all the time, but there was something urgent about this hooting, something forcing Meg's attention. It was nothing she could explain.

Not logically anyway.

Without further explanation Meg swiftly made her way outside at the same time as Mike, the porter. The car was tooting incessantly now, and Meg broke into a run. Pulling open the door, she looked at the terrified and shocked face of a young woman, her large pregnant bump immediately obvious.

'I'm bleeding.'

Looking down, Meg swallowed as she watched the bright patch of blood spreading over her dress.

'What's your name?'

'Debbie. Debbie Evans.'

'How many weeks are you, Debbie?'

'Thirty-three. I'm supposed to be going to my antenatal appointment.'

Turning, Meg addressed the porter, who was patiently awaiting her instructions. 'Mike, grab a trolley and call for some help.' Meg turned back to the woman. 'It's okay, Debbie, we're going to get you inside now.' A small crowd had gathered now, as

Meg got what further details she could from the pale woman.

'What have we got?' Flynn rushed the trolley forward

'Thirty-three weeks pregnant. She was on her way to the obstetrician when she started bleeding.'

'A lot?'

Meg gave him a worried nod as she made her way around to the passenger side. Slipping in beside Debbie, she undid her seatbelt, helping as much as she could from her end as the strong arms of Mike and Flynn gently lifted the woman onto the waiting trolley.

By the time Meg had extracted herself from the car the trolley had disappeared inside and, slightly breathless from exertion and nervous energy, she followed them, instantly going to Flynn's side to assist in taking blood and establishing IV access. Oxygen was already being given to the shocked woman, and Meg shouted her instructions in clear tones as Jess assisted. Carla, back from her coffee and hesitant at first, soon forgot her nerves and even ran an IV infusion of Hartmann's through the giving set, passing it to Meg as intravenous access was established.

'Good work,' Meg said encouragingly, without looking up.

'Debbie, my name is Flynn Kelsey. I'm the Emergency consultant.'

Passing Flynn the necessary tubes for an urgent FBE and cross match, Meg set up another flask of fluid as Jess appeared.

'Need a hand?' Mike was still discreetly hovering,

knowing he would soon be needed. As part of the Emergency team his role might not be hands-on, but his input was just as vital as the medical staff's if the department was going to run smoothly.

'Please, Mike. These bloods need to go, stat, as soon as Flynn signs off the form. Make sure the lab knows they're urgent.'

Picking up the telephone, Meg punched in the radiography department's number. 'It's Meg in Emergency. We need an urgent obstetric ultrasound in resus.' Meg paused.

Flynn was busy examining Debbie's abdomen. He felt the baby's position for a moment, before attempting to find the heartbeat with the Doppler machine Jess had just passed him. The tiniest collective sigh as a heartbeat was picked up made Meg realise she hadn't been the only one holding her breath.

'Your baby's got a good strong heartbeat.' Flynn's words were calm and assured and he held Debbie's gaze. For an instant Meg felt her mind flash back to the accident, and those same grey eyes as he told her she was safe, that everything was going to be okay. She watched Debbie relax a fraction, the utter fear in her face fade a touch. Flynn was certainly a good doctor; he managed to combine a relaxed bedside manner with an air of concentrated efficiency and direct honesty. 'But you are bleeding a lot, Debbie. I'm going to do an ultrasound to see exactly what's going on. Has anyone told you that your placenta is lying low?'

Debbie nodded. The loss of blood was making her drowsy. 'Stay with me, Debbie.' The same sharp voice he had used on Meg was dragging Debbie back to consciousness.

'I was going to have a Caesarean. Placenta pr...' Her voice trailed off and Meg watched as she closed her eyes.

'Come on, Debbie.' It was Meg speaking sharply now, forcing Debbie to stay awake as Flynn concentrated on the ultrasound.

'Placenta praevia,' Flynn said, confirming the assumed diagnosis. 'What's her blood pressure?'

'Eighty over fifty.'

'Will she be transferred to the maternity hospital?' Carla's voice was a loud whisper, and Flynn looked up and made his way over.

'Good question. But no. She needs to go straight to Theatre.'

Carla's eyes widened. 'But there's no Obstetrics here at Bayside.'

Flynn nodded 'If Mohammed won't go to the mountain...'

Carla gave him a completely nonplussed look.

'Meg will explain. Call me the second you're worried.' With a brief nod he left the room. Meg knew he would be on the telephone, safely out of earshot of Debbie.

'What was that about mountains?'

Meg grinned. 'The mountain will have to come to Mohammed. It's a saying. He'll be ringing the emergency obstetric team to hotfoot it over here.'

'They'll do the Caesarean in the Theatre here?'

Meg nodded.

The first unit of blood had arrived, along with a

breathless Mike, and Meg thanked him for his speedy work. As it required two qualified nurses to check it, Carla observed as Jess and Meg ran through the formalities, carefully checking the patient's identity badge with the corresponding number on the bag of blood. The painstaking checking was all the more essential now the patient was barely conscious.

'We're going to put the blood through the blood warmer,' Meg explained. 'This blood is cold, and as we want to transfuse her quickly this will warm it to body temperature.' She showed Carla the long coil inside the machine that would warm the blood. 'The usual obs apply—close checking of pulse, blood pressure and respirations—but variations due to the blood are harder to detect in someone so sick, as their obs are unstable anyway. Any rash or rise in temperature is of particular importance and must be reported immediately.'

'Debbie?' Flynn returned, the consent form in his hand. 'Debbie!'

Her eyes flicked open, too shocked and exhausted now to be scared. 'We need to perform an urgent Caesarean.'

'It's too soon.'

'Your baby has to be born.'

Debbie rallied a bit then, her maternal instinct forcing her to concentrate to stay awake and fight for her baby.

'It's too soon,' she repeated.

'There's no choice.' His words were forceful, yet gentle. 'Debbie, we have to get your baby out, for both your sakes. You're thirty-three weeks—it's early, but not impossibly so. Your baby really needs to be born.'

Meg watched with compassion. She knew so well how Debbie was feeling—that overwhelming urge to just close your eyes—yet Debbie was struggling to focus.

'Will you do it?' Debbie asked.

Flynn shook his head. 'No, the obstetric team are on their way. But if they don't get here in time and it becomes necessary then I will. I'm going to do everything I can for you and your baby.'

Her pale hand accepted the pen and, shaking, Debbie managed a weak signature on the paper.

'My husband…'

'We've contacted him, and he'll be sent straight up to Theatre when he gets here.'

Meg smiled at the woman and then looked up to Flynn. 'Shall we get her up?'

'Yep.'

Mike didn't need to be asked even once. He arranged the IV pole and the cardiac monitor onto the trolley and switched Debbie's oxygen piping over to the portable cylinder as Meg collected the emergency boxes containing drugs and resuscitation equipment.

If Debbie suddenly went off *en-route* the safest thing would probably be just to carry on running as, realistically speaking, Theatre was her only chance. But, as Flynn had only so recently pointed out, oxygenated blood was vital for Debbie and her baby. Slipping an airway and ambu bag under Debbie's pillow, silently hoping she wouldn't need to use them,

Meg made a final quick check that everything was in order.

Going out with the Mobile Accident Unit was probably the most exciting thing in Emergency—the kick of adrenaline as you pulled on your gear, the call of the unknown as the ambulance drove off with sirens wailing, running through blood, checking equipment *en-route*, the crackling details coming in over the ambulance radio. But running through a busy hospital at high speed—curious stares, the lift held as you dashed past, the rush of excitement a true crisis generated in an Emergency nurse's stomach—well, usually that came a close second.

But not today.

Today Meg was just desperately concerned for her patient and the unborn baby. All she wanted was to get them to Theatre—get her patient the help she needed. It was as if a light had gone off inside her: the adrenaline buzz that emergency nurses survived on just wasn't happening for Meg as they ran along the corridor. And run they did. Flynn gave them no choice, his long legs making the dash seem effortless. It was all right for him, Meg grumbled to herself as they stood in the lift. Meg was struggling to catch her breath while Flynn stood there calmly eyeing the cardiac monitor. It was all right for him, *he* didn't have a ribcage that felt like a used football.

'All right Meg?'

'Couldn't be better,' she answered dryly as the lift door opened and the mad dash to Theatre started again.

But there was no rushing once they stepped into

the hallowed grounds of the theatre. Here the staff were never ruffled, were almost relaxed, even, as they accepted the patient and lifted her over onto the operating table. Everything was in place already—the resuscitation cot in the corner of the room, the packs being opened. No one would have guessed that an emergency Caesarean hadn't been performed in the small theatre for well over two years. Theatre, like Emergency, had to be prepared for every eventuality.

'We'll take it from here, thank you.' The theatre sister smiled as the anaesthetist appeared. 'The team's just arrived and they're on their way up.'

Which was a rather polite way of telling the trio to leave. But they didn't want to; Meg could sense even Flynn's reluctance. There was a baby here about to be born. Debbie was their patient, and letting go was sometimes hard.

'Can Carla stay? She's a student.' It was worth a try—Meg knew it would be great experience for her.

The theatre sister hesitated for an age. 'Show her where to change—but she has to stay at the back of the room.'

Meg grinned widely. 'She will. Thanks.'

Carla was so excited Meg practically had to dress her. 'Here's your blues. Come on, Carla, quickly or you'll miss it. Now, just grab some clogs—they'll do—and tuck your hair into this hat. If you think Jess is strict, wait till you meet the theatre sister! Now, *come on.*'

Pushing her through the black swing doors, Meg just managed to call out, 'Good luck!' and then she was gone.

'That was nice of you.'

Looking up, she was both surprised and embarrassed to see Flynn waiting for her to walk back to Emergency.

'Asking if Carla could stay—she'll really enjoy it.'

Meg realised she was frowning. Just what was it with those two? 'Just so long as she doesn't faint.'

'Oh, she won't. She's been hanging out to get into Theatre for ages.'

Meg felt her frown deepen. Since when did consultants take such an interest in nursing students? Silly question, Meg realised with a stab of disappointment. Especially when you didn't want to know the answer. 'It will be good experience for her,' she replied in efficient tones. 'She's only in her second year, so she hasn't done Theatre yet. You can pore over the books, but nothing beats it first-hand.'

'Absolutely.'

'I had an ulterior motive,' Meg admitted. 'At least I'll get a first-hand, in-depth report of what happened—not some cool message from Theatre.' He didn't respond, and they walked along in silence, flattening themselves against the corridor as a team pushing a huge incubator rushed past them. 'There's the mobile PICU,' Meg observed. 'They made good time as well.'

'Meg?' They were still standing against the wall and Meg turned, hearing the serious note in his voice. 'About that kiss…'

'What about it?' Meg replied airily, setting off at twice their previous pace.

'Don't you think we ought to talk about it?'

Meg gave a scornful laugh. 'Why? Are you worried I'm going to dash off to Personnel and squeal sexual harassment?'

'No.'

'Then forget it.' She even managed to shrug. 'I'm not expecting you to follow it up with a marriage proposal. It was just a kiss—a bit of fun.'

She was lying through her teeth. It had been far more than a bit of fun for Meg—her lips were still scorching from his touch—but she certainly wasn't going to let Flynn see the effect he'd had on her. Unless one of them handed their notice in they were going to be seeing a lot of each other, and she was determined not to let him see how his reckless bit of fun had sent her into a spin.

'When do you think they'll transfer Debbie to the maternity hospital?'

It was a pointless question, an obvious attempt to change the subject, and Meg felt herself flush. Verbal diarrhoea wasn't a condition she usually suffered from.

'This afternoon, I guess, once she's a bit more sta-ble. She's lucky she got to us. Heaven knows how she didn't have an accident, given the state she was in when she arrived.'

'Oh, well, at least you'll have time before she goes to give her a quick lecture on the dangers of driving while haemorrhaging.' It was a cheap shot, but she was still smarting at the harsh way he had spoken to her when she was a patient. Again Flynn didn't answer. 'So what do you reckon the baby's chances are?'

Flynn pondered for a moment before answering. 'Good,' he said finally, and Meg rolled her eyes.

'That's it?'

She watched his eyebrows furrow. 'What did you want me to say?'

Meg shrugged. 'Good, I guess, but a bit of padding would be nice.'

'I'm not one for small talk.'

'Well, you could have fooled me. You never stopped talking when I had my accident, and you hardly hold back with the students.'

Flynn shrugged. 'So I don't treat the students like a bunch of gormless subordinates. It is the twenty-first century, you know, and as for the accident...' It was Flynn stepping up the pace now, striding off down the highly polished corridor, forcing Meg to half run to keep up with him. 'It was my job to keep you awake.'

Which should have made her cheeks scorch—but something stirred inside Meg. Something akin to anger. 'And was it "your job" to dress me down in the obs ward?'

Flynn didn't seem remotely fazed by her accusatory tones. With a wry smile he finally slowed down and, turning, caught her eye. They had arrived at the emergency department now and he held the door for her as they entered. 'No,' he admitted. But her victory was short-lived when he continued, 'That was more a moral duty.'

For once the place was deserted and Jess greeted them with a smile. 'Why don't you grab a coffee, Meg, before I head off for my meeting?'

'Good idea,' Flynn answered, and, silently fuming, Meg followed his broad back around to the staff room.

Sitting down, she slipped off her shoes as Flynn headed straight for the kettle. 'White with one,' she said cheekily, and as he turned around with the kettle in his hand Meg gave him a smile. 'Oh, sorry, Flynn. Didn't I tell you? I'm not one for small talk.'

Okay, so the earth didn't move. Meg didn't suddenly become the social butterfly of the Emergency Department and Flynn didn't roar with laughter and crack open a packet of chocolate biscuits. But he *did* make her a coffee, and he did sit on the same side of the room as her and ask how she felt she was coping on for her first morning back after her accident.

'Better now.'

'Is my coffee that good, then?'

Meg stood up and spooned another teaspoon of sugar into her cup, and just to annoy him added a touch more coffee. 'No. I meant that I finally feel back in the saddle, so to speak. I know I've only been off a couple of weeks but it seems much longer.'

He turned then to the television, and for something to do Meg gazed unseeing at the screen. 'What was it like for you? I heard you did research for a couple of years before you took up this post.'

'That's right.' He took a long sip of his coffee before continuing. 'It was a bit hard, I guess,' he admitted finally. 'It still is.' There was something in his voice that made Meg look over, that told her she had just hit upon a raw nerve.

'In what way?'

'Four pounds two, with eyes of blue.' Carla burst into the staff room brimming with excitement, her smile so infectious even Flynn's suddenly serious face broke into a grin.

'What did she have?' Meg immediately asked.

'A little boy. He's so tiny, but just beautiful. Thanks so much for asking if I could stay, Meg. It was just amazing—and so quick!'

'Sit down. I'll get you a coffee—I reckon you've earned it!' Meg laughed. 'How's Debbie doing?'

'Well, they're stitching her up, and the sister said that she'd be in Recovery for a while before they transferred her, but the anaesthetist said to tell you, Flynn—' another blush crept across Carla's face as she addressed him '—that they're happy with her obs and she's haemo…haemodynamically stable now.'

'That's good. Ideally we would have liked to transfer Debbie with the baby in utero—there's no better incubator than the mother. But in this case we had no choice but to deliver there and then…'

Meg watched as he went into detail, patiently explaining the merits and pitfalls of the crucial choice he had made that morning in resus. And though he spoke about nothing but the patient, though he was nothing but friendly and professional, Meg couldn't help but notice how easily and readily he chatted with the student. How familiar they seemed with each other. And, more pointedly, even if she had wanted to, Meg couldn't miss the rapt expression on Carla's face, the flirty way she looked up at him from under her eyelashes.

There was something going on here that Meg didn't quite understand. And what was more, Meg realised as she left them to it and slipped away unnoticed, she wasn't entirely sure that she wanted to.

CHAPTER FOUR

'ANYONE there catch your eye?' Kathy breezed into the living room and Meg hastily put down the guest list she had been stealing a look at.

'There must be a hundred names there!' Meg exclaimed.

'I'm sure Mum can stretch to one hundred and one if there's someone I've missed out.' Kathy's voice was loaded with innuendo and Meg deliberately chose to ignore it.

'I'm sure there's enough there to be going on with.'

There was. The one name Meg was interested in— Flynn's name—was right there near the top. Unfortunately Kathy had listed the guests randomly, so there was no way of telling if the 'Maria' above his name or the 'Louise' below it was his partner. And more worrying was the utter relief she felt that Carla's name most definitely wasn't there. But if she asked Kathy, Meg might just as well take out a full-page advertisement in the local paper telling the world she had a crush on Flynn Kelsey.

A bit more than a crush, Meg admitted to herself reluctantly, but she wasn't in any rush to give her heart away again—and certainly not to someone so effortlessly divine, so overtly charismatic as Flynn Kelsey. After all, hadn't she left her last job because of a disastrous relationship? Even though Vince hadn't worked with her, his infidelity had permeated her workplace. A casual fling—and Meg thought glumly that that was all it would be to Flynn—was a recipe for disaster. It wasn't just her heart she had to look out for either, her resumé simply wasn't up to another update. Inevitably it would end in tears— most probably hers—and three jobs in six months wasn't a record Meg wanted to achieve.

And yet...

In the past few weeks Meg had found herself glancing at the medical staff's roster with more than a passing interest, and to her dying shame had agreed to an overtime shift just because Flynn was on duty. And though she loved working with him, adored the constant verbal sparring, the undeniable flirting, each shift was tempered with a sense of frustration, a need to finish whatever it was they had both started, to somehow let them draw their own natural conclusion.

Flynn Kelsey was more to Meg than just another colleague, and to deny it would be an outright lie.

'What are you daydreaming about?'

Meg shook her head. 'Nothing.' How she would love to confide in Kathy—ask her for some insight, find out once and for all if she was wasting her time. Contrary to what Flynn had said about Kathy playing matchmaker, Flynn's name had never even been brought up once. But Meg knew her sister only too well, and subtle certainly wasn't her middle name. If Meg even remotely asked about him, and *if* Flynn did turn out to be single, Kathy would think nothing of seizing the day and engineering a dance or three at the party, or some quiet little dinner with Flynn and

Meg making up the numbers—by chance, of course! That was the sort of help she could do without. It was far safer all round to keep quiet and steer the conversation back to the party and the wedding.

'I know that look.' Kathy picked up the list. 'Come on, Meg, surely someone there catches your eye? What about Lee—six foot two, blue eyes…?'

'I don't think I'm ready for a man with three kids,' Meg said dryly.

'Okay, point taken. How about Harry, then? At least he comes without baggage, and he's a plastic surgeon so he must be loaded.'

Meg gave a cynical laugh. 'He's certainly not loaded with personality.'

'So you want personality *and* a clean slate?' She ran her eye down the paper. 'Well, that rules out just about everyone here. Looks like you'll be dancing round your handbag with me and Mum.'

'You'll be with Jake, remember?'

Kathy poked out her tongue. 'Jake's the last person I'll be dancing with; he might be gorgeous to look at, but, believe me, propped up at the bar is the best place for him; dancing really isn't his forte.'

'That's right; I'd forgotten! Do you remember when Vince and Jake got up and danced at that night-club? The bouncers thought they were drunk and they'd only been on orange juice all night.'

'Oh, my goodness.' Kathy blinked slowly a couple of times, her face breaking into a grin. 'That's the first time I've heard you mention Vince without getting that misty look in your eyes.'

Meg nodded. 'I'm *so* over him, Kathy. That accident was probably the best thing that ever happened to me. Hanging upside down in a smashed up car is a pretty good reminder of how precious life is, and a couple of weeks licking my wounds, with an excuse to cry if I wanted to, was just the tonic I needed. Vince could walk through the door this moment and tell me he's left his wife and I'd just promptly show him the way out. I've wasted enough of my time on him.'

'Well, good for you.' Kathy's beaming smile belied the trace of doubt in her voice, but Meg homed in on it straight away.

'I'm over him,' Meg insisted.

Kathy put her hands up in mock defence. 'I believe you! And to prove it, how about I treat you to a glass of champagne to celebrate the demise of "bloody Vince"? There's a new wine bar just opened on the Bay Road...'

'Not for me. I'm on a late shift.'

'Well, an iced coffee, then? I need to get some shoes for the party. I could really use your opinion.'

Meg shook her head. 'When did you ever need my opinion on anything? Anyway, you know I can't walk in a shoe shop without buying something. I've already spent enough on my dress—speaking of which, that's why I'm here. I'm heading off to the beach to get a bit of sun; I'm so pale you can't tell where the fabric ends and my legs start. Look, tell Mum I'm sorry I missed her. I'll pop back for a shower before I go to work, but tell her I've already eaten or she'll be warming up the soup in the freezer!'

'If you don't stay for lunch you know she'll moan

that you're using the house as a beach hut again?'
Kathy warned

'I'll risk it.' Grabbing her bag from the couch, Meg
gave her sister a cheery wave and, savouring the delicious morning, walked the couple of hundred yards
from her parents' house to the beach.

Slipping off her sarong, Meg laid it on the sand
before stretching out luxuriously on it. Closing her
eyes, she waited for the little dots dancing before her
eyes to fade, wriggling her toes into the warm sand
and feeling the heat of the late morning sun bathing
her body. This was the best time of year to be at the
beach; apart from a couple of mothers with young
children, and a few older couples strolling along, the
place was practically deserted. It would be a different
story in two weeks' time, when the schools broke up
for the summer break. Then she would have to share
the beach with seemingly hundreds of screaming children and overwrought parents, but for now it was
pretty near perfect.

Perfect, even.

An alarm clock would be good, though, Meg
thought as she drifted off, her mind flicking back for
a moment to her accident, remembering Flynn beside
her, holding her hand as they waited for the firefighters to secure the tree, imagining the sound of the
ocean. It was almost a pleasant memory, made better
because this time she could close her eyes, this time
she could sleep…

At first Meg felt only relief when a child's screams
dragged her awake. Focussing on her watch, she stood
up with a yelp and shook the sand out of her sarong.

Never mind the soup, there wouldn't even be time for a shower at this rate. Fuzzy from sleep, and the bright midday sun, it took Meg a second or two to register that the screaming hadn't stopped—in fact it had multiplied. A woman was screaming.

Loudly.

Swinging around, Meg watched in horror as she saw a woman running hysterically along the beach, twisting and turning, carrying a screaming child in her arms.

A bleeding child.

That second was all it took for Meg to break into a run, to shout her orders to the stunned onlookers who were watching helplessly, frozen with shock.

'Get me a towel. Someone call for an ambulance.'

The screaming grew louder, and Meg acknowledged with relief that the child was screaming also as the woman practically threw the infant into her arms. 'He stood on a bottle. Oh, God—help him, please!'

'It's all right, darling.' Despite her own fear Meg spoke soothingly to the child. Lying him down, she immediately raised his leg. The blood was pouring from his foot. Meg swallowed hard. It wasn't pouring; it was pumping. He had a large arterial bleed. Immediately she applied pressure behind his knee, holding the leg as high as she could as an elderly gentleman thrust a towel at her.

'Here—can you use this?'

'I can't let go of his leg.'

'Tell me what you want me to do.'

Meg nodded, relief washing over her. Her fear was real. Nothing scared her in Emergency—there she knew what she was doing, could put her hand on the necessary equipment in an instant, summon help at the touch of a button or the buzz of an intercom. But here she was on her own. Apart from this man no one had done a single thing to help—all were standing uselessly. Meg didn't blame them for a moment, but it didn't help matters in the least. But this man was sensible. The sweat was pouring off him, and there was a grey tinge to his lips, but he was at least listening, ready to help. 'Hold his leg up and push like I am behind his knee. I need to have a look before I wrap it up.'

As soon as Meg released the pressure the blood started spurting again. By now the child had stopped screaming; he was lying there shocked and pale, which worried Meg far more than the noise.

'Has someone called for an ambulance?' she asked as she examined the foot. There was no glass visible so, taking the towel, she wrapped it tightly around the foot, pulling it as hard as she could in an attempt to stem the flow of blood. 'Has someone called an ambulance yet?'

One of the women was frantically pushing the buttons on her mobile. 'It isn't charged.'

'Has anyone else got a mobile?'

'I could run up to one of the houses,' the man offered. Meg looked down at the child. He was becoming drowsy, and despite her best efforts already the towel was bright red. 'Or my car's just there. My wife could drive…'

Meg did a swift calculation. By the time he had run up, and assuming he got straight in to someone's house, it would be at least another ten minutes until the ambulance got here—and that was if their luck was in. If they dashed to a car she could have him straight in within five minutes.

'We'll go by car. I have to keep pushing—keep his leg up.'

He nodded. 'June—go and start the car.'

Spurred into action, the assembled crowd finally moved, helping to carry the boy the short distance along the beach to the waiting car. The mother sat in the front, sobbing loudly as Meg and her helper squeezed into the back and the car jerked away.

'Drive carefully,' Meg warned the woman.

'But step on it, love.' The man gave Meg a small smile. 'She's as slow as a snail normally. My name's Roland.'

'Meg.'

It was only a short drive, and even as the car pulled away Meg instantly felt calmer. Everything would be fine now. The hospital was in sight, and by emergency standards this wasn't particularly serious—not in the controlled setting of a hospital anyway.

'Thank goodness you were there.' The woman had stopped sobbing now, and was swallowing hard to compose herself.

'What's your son's name?'

'Toby. I'm Rita.'

Meg smiled down at the little boy as the car pulled into the ambulance bay. 'We'll have you sorted in no time, Toby.

'June, grab a trolley from the entrance and bring it up to the car,' Meg instructed. But Mike the porter, grabbing a quick smoke between jobs, had already beaten her to it. Pulling the back door open, he popped his head in. 'Here you go, Meg—anything I can do to help?'

'We just need him on the trolley, but I'll have to keep his leg up and the pressure on.'

'No worries.'

Anywhere else they would have looked a curious sight—four adults dressed in their bathers pushing a trolley with a bleeding child—but here at the Bayside Hospital they barely merited a second glance.

'You're starting your shift a bit early!' Jess joked. 'You really can't stay away from the place, can you?'

'I was supposed to be topping up my tan,' Meg groaned. 'It's pretty deep,' she added in low tones, so as not to frighten Toby and his mother. 'Arterial bleed. He lost a lot of blood at the beach.'

'Right.' Jess nodded, bandaging a huge wad of Combine firmly into place and elevating the foot of the trolley, then taking over pressing behind Toby's knee. 'We'll not disturb it until the doctor gets here. Speaking of which…' She turned and smiled as Flynn entered.

'What have we got here?' He barely glanced in Meg's direction, his eyes firmly fixed on Toby. 'You've been down at the beach, I see, young man.'

'I stood on a broken bottle.' It was the first time Toby had spoken, and Meg smiled at the little lisping voice.

'There was blood everywhere; he must have lost a gallon.' This was a slight exaggeration from Rita, but Meg nodded.

'He did lose a lot—the bleed's arterial. I stopped it with popliteal and direct pressure and we've kept it elevated.'

'Good.' Still his eyes stayed fixed on his young charge. 'Toby, I'm going to put a little needle into the back of your hand so I can give you some medicine to take away the pain. It will only hurt for a second. I know that you've been so brave up to now—can I ask you to be brave for just a moment longer?'

Toby nodded, but his mother wasn't convinced. 'Can't you numb it first? He hates needles.'

'He'll be fine,' Flynn said confidently. 'Numbing it would take twenty minutes or so to take effect, and I'd like to give him some fluid thorugh a drip and take some blood. He looks a bit shocked, and I'm sure he'd appreciate something to settle him before we take the dressing down.'

But Rita wanted an anaesthetic. 'He'll scream the place down.'

Meg watched Flynn's shoulders stiffen a fraction. The only person who was getting upset was Toby's mum, and if she carried on Toby was likely to start getting anxious again.

'Look, Rita,' Meg suggested, 'why don't we go and grab a cool drink and let the doctor get on with it? It must be very upsetting for you to watch all this.'

'Surely it would be better if I stayed?'

Meg took a deep breath. Honesty was the best policy, and all that, but she wasn't sure how well it was going to be received. 'It's probably better if we go and get a drink and calm down. The drip will be up by the time we get back and you'll feel a lot better then.'

Rita seemed to accept this, and after a rather tearful kiss and hug with Toby allowed herself to be led away.

'Is there anyone you'd like to ring?' Meg offered once they were in the staff room. Given that both women were dressed in their bathers, apart from the skimpy sarong wrapped around Meg, the waiting room hadn't seemed an appropriate place to send Rita. Anyway, Meg was desperate for a long cool drink and was sure Rita could use one.

'Just my husband—he's going to have a fit when I tell him.' Her hand was shaking as she picked up the telephone. 'Do you think Toby will need an operation?'

'Yes.' Meg said simply. 'It wouldn't be fair on Toby to try and repair it under local anaesthetic. Do you want me to dial for you?'

Rita nodded. 'Useless, aren't I?'

Meg shook her head. 'Don't say that. You're his mum; you're allowed to be upset.'

As predicted, Toby's dad didn't take the news too well, and after Rita had ducked off to the toilet for another quick cry Meg took the opportunity to ring her mother. Mary wasn't in the best of moods either.

'You just can't stay away from trouble, can you? And you haven't even had lunch. How can you do a full shift without a morsel of food in your stomach and no work clothes?'

'I've got some spare shoes here, and I can wear Theatre gear. I'll be fine,' Meg assured her.

'Fine, my foot.' Not the greatest choice of words. 'I'll bring you up a Thermos of soup.'

'Please, Mum, don't bother. I'm okay. Honestly,' she added, but with zero effect.

'Tell that to the patients when you're fainting over them. I'll warm it up and bring it straight over. Do you need anything else?'

Meg looked down at her blood-splattered sarong and her sand-dusted legs. 'A toiletry bag would be nice.'

'I'm on my way.'

'Where's Rita?' Jess popped her head around the door.

'In the loo. How's Toby doing?'

'He's going straight up to Theatre. The plastics had a quick look and they want to get him up now. They need her to come and sign the consent form. How are you?'

Meg stood up. 'Desperate for a shower. If my mum comes can you ask her just to drop all my stuff in the changing room? I'll be round to start my shift when I'm looking a bit more presentable.'

'Sure. Take your time, Meg. I reckon you've earned it.'

Rita appeared then, and Meg left them to it. Her shift hadn't even started and already she felt as if she'd done a day's work.

'There you are.' Flynn loomed into view. 'Where's Toby's mother? The plastics need her to—'

'Sign the consent,' Meg finished for him. 'I know—Jess is already onto it. I'm just heading off for a shower.'

'Oh.' For the first time since her arrival he actually managed to look at her, his eyes flicking down her body. For the last half-hour Meg had been wandering around barefoot, her modesty protected only by a sheer sunflower-emblazoned sarong, yet totally unabashed. Now, under Flynn's scrutiny, she suddenly felt exposed and woefully inadequately dressed.

'There wasn't really time to get changed first,' Meg joked feebly.

'Of course not.'

His eyes were looking somewhere at the top of her forehead as he cleared his throat, and Meg could have sworn that the beginning of a blush was creeping over his usually deadpan face. She should have gone then—nodded politely and dashed to the refuge of the changing rooms. But for some reason her legs simply wouldn't obey her and she stood there mute, staring back at him, forcing his eyes to meet hers.

'How was the beach—before all this happened, I mean?'

'Wonderful.'

Something strange was going on. Something strange and delicious. An apparently sedate, normal conversation was taking place, but there was nothing normal about the white-hot look passing between them, and definitely nothing sedate about the pulse flickering relentlessly between her thighs or the sudden swell of her nipples, jutting against the flimsy fabric of her sarong, inching their way closer to Flynn with a will of their own.

His hand moved up to her face. Meg didn't flinch, just stood there. The pad of his thumb gently brushed

across her cheek. 'You've got sand on your face.' Her
instinct was to reach up and capture his hand, to hold
it against her cheek and then guide it down slowly to
her aching engorged breasts. But there was nothing
she could do except stand there, terrified she might
be misreading the blazing signs, painfully aware that
a hospital corridor wasn't the best place to make a
complete fool of yourself if sand was the only thing
on his mind.

'Thank you,' she said simply, the tension unbearable. 'I'd best get on.'

The changing room was only a few steps away but
it seemed to stretch on for ever.

'Meg?'

She turned slowly, not trusting herself to speak.

'I'm looking forward to the party on Saturday.'

Meg nodded, gripping onto the door handle for
dear life. 'Me too,' she managed to croak, and, attempting a nonchalant exit, waited until the changing
room door was safely closed before slipping onto a
wooden bench and resting her burning face in her
hands.

How was she going to survive the afternoon, let
alone last until Saturday?

Of course the one time Meg really wanted to be busy
and appear professional, the department was practically deserted. Toby was cleared out quickly, and
apart from a couple of gastros and the usual lumps
and bumps they remained frustratingly quiet.

'Come on, Carla, we can practise your BLS on
Annie.'

'Oh, spare her, Meg—the poor lass spent two hours with her this morning,' Jess responded cheerfully. 'She's probably seen Annie more than her boyfriend this week, haven't you, Carla?'

'Actually, I haven't got a boyfriend.'

'What? A pretty young thing like you?' Jess clucked. 'Surely there must be some young man you've got your eye on.'

Carla shrugged, but not before her cheeks darkened, and Meg watched her gaze flick over to Flynn, who was obliviously writing notes in the corner of the annexe.

'Well, there must be some cupboards that need to be sorted,' Meg said quickly, before Jess followed Carla's gaze.

'All done—by my own fair hands. Now, why don't you go and have your afternoon tea? And maybe for once the early shift can get out on time—though I've probably just jinxed myself and there'll be a busload pulling up now.'

'Well, if we're expecting a rush on...' Flynn recapped his fountain pen '...I might get myself something from the machine to tide me over.'

Jess clapped her hand to her forehead. 'That reminds me—the machine's not working, I'd best ring the canteen.'

The kitchen seemed to have shrunk to minuscule proportions as Meg attempted to make coffee. The brief display of affection, the reference to Saturday— all seemed to be crackling in the air around them as Flynn opened the fridge and pulled out a rather sad-looking yellow jelly. 'Not exactly what I had in mind.'

Meg screwed her nose up. 'Yuk—*and* it's diabetic jelly,' she added, looking at the hospital canteen label.

'Any bread in the bread bin?'

'What? At three o'clock? We're right at the end of the food chain, bar the night staff.'

Even the cornflakes box was empty.

It was only then that Meg remembered her mother had dropped her off some supplies. Knowing Mary, there would be enough to feed a small third world country. She dashed off to the changing room and returned triumphant with a large thermo bag packed full with a flask and a mountain of sandwiches. 'At least some of us come prepared,' she said, depositing the bag on the kitchen bench. 'Help yourself.'

'What's this?' Flynn asked, opening the bag with all the relish of a child on Christmas morning.

Why Meg fibbed at this point she never knew. What she hoped to gain by having Flynn think she was a whiz in the kitchen not only eluded her, it also belied all Meg's feminist principles. But the small white lie was out before she could stop it. 'Just some soup and sandwiches I made.'

'Great.' Pulling out the shiny foil packages, he turned casually. 'What's in them?'

It was an obvious question and one, to Meg's dying shame, she realised she couldn't answer. Ignoring him, Meg concentrated on spooning sugar into two mugs.

'What's in the sandwiches?' Flynn persisted.

'I don't know,' she responded, flustered. 'Ham,

cheese—whatever was in the fridge. It's hardly decision of the day!'

'I only asked,' he muttered, carrying them through to the staff room as Meg followed with the drinks.

Just as they started eating Jess appeared. 'Oh, you found them. Flynn *did* remember to tell you that your mum had dropped off your lunch—I thought he might have forgotten.'

'This chicken's just delicious, Meg,' Flynn said with a mischievous glint in his eye as he took a huge bite. 'You must give me the recipe.'

Jess flashed him a quizzical look. 'Nice to see a man who enjoys cooking. Now, Flynn, this lass with the ulcer in cubicle three—did you want me to use Comfeel or Aquacel for her dressing? You didn't write it on the cas card.'

'Oh, I don't know,' Flynn quipped, grinning at his own warped humour. 'Comfeel, Aquacel—whatever's on the dressing trolley. You choose, Jess. After all, it's hardly decision of the day.'

As a slightly bemused Jess wandered off Meg picked up a magazine and pretended to read, ignoring his grin.

'Great sandwiches.'

'So you've already said.'

'What's in the flask?'

'Soup—help yourself.' Meg looked up. 'And, no, I didn't make it.' Turning her eyes back to the magazine, Meg pretended to be engrossed in an article about the latest Hollywood scandal.

'No, thanks. I'm not a fan of soup.'

Meg didn't respond, just carried on pretending to read, her cheeks still flaming.

'These will tide me over. I might head off to the new wine bar on the beach front tonight; it's supposed to be good. Have you tried it?'

'No.' Why couldn't he leave her alone to die of shame quietly?

'What time do you finish tonight?'

The blush that had only just started to recede was coming back for an encore.

'Nine-thirty,' she responded, as casually as she could with her heart in her mouth. Surely this wasn't what it sounded like?

'Do you fancy joining me?'

Turning the page of her magazine, she found a glossy supermodel grinning back at her, brown, lithe and with an overabundance of self-confidence.

'I would,' Meg said lightly, though her heart was doing somersaults. 'Except I don't think I'd get in in a bikini and blood-stained sarong.'

'Oh, I don't know.' Flynn laughed. 'The dress code's supposed to be pretty laid-back. Still, we could stop at your place if you want to get changed.' Standing, he screwed up the tin foil and casually tossed it into the bin. 'How about it?'

Her resolve was weakening—the threat of changing her resumé a poor argument in the face of such delicious provocation. It was only a drink, Meg reasoned, and after all lots of nurses moved around. If the worst came to the worst she could always join an agency.

The clock was ticking as Meg wrestled with her

conscience, and she knew that if she didn't answer quickly then Flynn might realise the profoundness of his invitation. 'Okay,' she answered, in such a voice that would make even the laid-back Carla sound edgy. 'Sounds good.'

'Great, I'll catch up on some paperwork, then. Give me a knock on my office door when your shift finishes.' And he strolled out of the room as if he'd just asked her to drop by a pile of admission notes.

The supermodel was still grinning at her, and Meg found she was grinning back.

An evening with Flynn Kelsey.

Now, what girl could ask for more?

CHAPTER FIVE

SHAVING your legs with a disposable hospital razor could be risky at the best of times. But shaving them in a handbasin with a heart-rate topping one hundred and hands shaking with nervous anticipation was a feat in itself, particularly as she was only supposed to be nipping out to the loo for five minutes. Eying the shaky lock, Meg debated whether to risk shaving under her arms.

Stop it, she warned herself. It's just a casual drink, and even if it was a date—a real date—she was hardly going to rip off her clothes and jump into bed with him.

Hardly.

Tossing the plastic razor into the bin, Meg took a deep breath. Gorgeous he might be—stunning, even—but she was on the rebound, just getting over a broken heart, and more to the point casual sex simply wasn't her style.

Yet...

There was nothing casual about Meg's feelings for Flynn. Since the day she had met him, since those moments trapped in her car, there had been an attraction—an undeniable attraction. The kiss they had shared hadn't been an accident, hadn't been a passing whim. It had been an inevitable consequence—a necessary outlet for the pressure cooker of steam that

seemed to build up whenever they were thrown together. The occasional bickering, the sometimes
stilted conversations, were more an attempt to stem
the tide, to defuse the atmosphere, than a sign of in-
compatibility. And now they were finally doing something about it.

Who knows? Meg tried to reason. After a glass of
wine he might not look so appealing—and if that was
the case at least they'd know. But then again, Meg
thought with a fluttering excitement that gnawed at
the very pinnacle of her being, suppose things did
move on? Suppose by the time the last drinks were
served, the attraction was still most defiantly
mutual…?

Mary O'Sullivan must have thought someone was
walking over her grave as Meg rummaged guiltily
through the bin and retrieved the razor. Her mother
would never understand, Meg realised, but then how
could she be expected to, when Meg herself didn't
understand the feelings Flynn Kelsey ignited in her?
How six months of steely resolve and heartfelt resolution could so easily be discarded by the crook of
his little finger…

'All finished?'

Meg nodded. She'd been willing the shift to pass,
but now the time had come suddenly she longed for
the relative comfort of work, half hoped Flynn's pager
would go off and there would be a legitimate excuse
to end whatever they had started here and now. But
his pager didn't go off, and it was a tentative, nervous

Meg that walked quietly alongside him out to the car park.

'Flynn!'

The voice calling out in the darkness made them both jump a fraction, but, seeing Carla rushing towards them, Flynn instantly relaxed.

'Carla, what's wrong?'

'The car.'

Flynn groaned. 'Again? You're going to have to do something about it, you know.'

'I know,' Carla replied breathlessly, eyeing Meg with some suspicion. 'Look, sorry—I didn't realise you were on your way somewhere. I can call out the breakdown services.'

'That's okay,' Meg finally found her voice. Suspicious of Carla's motives she might be, but acting all proprietary when they hadn't been for so much as a drink together wasn't her style, and anyway, fanning the flames of the hospital grapevine was the last thing she needed after her time at Melbourne City. 'Flynn was just giving me a ride home. Given what happened with Toby at the beach, I'm a bit stranded today.'

In an instant the slightly petulant expression that had been marring Carla's usually pretty face vanished. 'Of course.'

Handing Meg his keys, Flynn pointed to a rather impressive silver sports car. 'Meg, why don't you wait in the car? It's a bit cooler. I'll just see if I can work my magic on Carla's pile of junk.' He winked at Carla as if sharing an old joke. 'Again.'

Meg sat there trying desperately to relax. She

watched him hunched over the bonnet, watched Carla leaning against it, tossing her shaggy blonde hair, her little bust jutting out of the skimpy top she was wearing, and just knew that it wasn't an outfit Carla had casually thrown on after her shift.

When Carla slipped into the driving seat Meg rolled her eyes and gave a cynical snort as, lo and behold, the car started first time.

'Sorry about that.' Grinning, slightly breathless, Flynn slid in the car beside her.

'What was wrong with it?'

'Search me. It's happened a couple of times. I've told her to get it seen to.'

'Flynn?' The single word was out before she could stop it and she watched as he turned to her, a searching look on his face. 'There's nothing wrong with her car.'

'Meg, it's a pile of junk. It's no wonder it's always breaking down.'

'So it's happened a few times?'

She watched his hands grip hard on the steering wheel and wished she could somehow retrieve the words that had just slipped out of her mouth, take back the accusing, slightly jealous tone that had crept into her voice.

'Yes, it's happened a few times. And for the record, your honour—' he was trying to make a joke, but neither of them were smiling '—Carla's father is an old colleague of mine. I know her family well.'

'You don't have to explain. I mean, I wasn't suggesting...' Her voice trailed off and she felt like opening the car door and making a bolt for it. The night was ruined and they hadn't even left the car park yet!

'I know you weren't.' His voice was softer now, and when Meg looked up she realised he was smiling at her. 'How about we make a move? I've still got to stop for petrol, and at this rate we'll be lucky to make it for last orders at the bar.'

'Sounds good.' Meg forced herself to smile back, and as he started the engine and the car slid off she leant back in the soft leather seat, willing herself to loosen up, to relax. But she couldn't. All their sparkling repartee, the backchat and witty answers, seemed to have vanished, and they drove in uncomfortable silence for the next couple of kilometres.

'I'd better stop at this garage or it will be me calling out the breakdown services.'

'Sure.'

'Do you want anything?'

Meg shook her head, letting out a rather strained breath as he closed the door. God, he was probably wondering what had possessed him to ask her, she thought as he filled the car with petrol. The forecourt was bright, and Meg watched as he strode across to pay. His wallet sitting on the dashboard caught her eye about two seconds after Flynn started patting at his pocket, and she held it up as he grinned and beckoned her over.

Maybe it was nerves, or just her rush to fetch it for him, but as she dropped his wallet on the forecourt Meg felt as if her world had suddenly ended. The photo Flynn kept in his wallet was smiling back at her. There, younger, a touch slimmer, but unmistakably him, stood Flynn—and Jake too, for that matter. Both men were smiling happily, not a care in the world, their arms wrapped around the woman between them.

The *bride* between them.

And from the adoration in Flynn's eyes Meg knew that the bride was his.

Flynn was walking towards her, calling her name as his eyes darted from the open wallet in her hands back to her stricken face.

'When were you going to tell me?' She threw it at him. 'After you'd taken me out? Or were you going to sleep with me first?'

'Meg, I can explain.'

'I'm sure you can.' Her voice was rising and people were starting to look, but she didn't care. 'What? Doesn't your wife understand you? Come on, Flynn, try me. But I can guarantee I've heard it before.'

'Meg, just listen, will you…?' He grabbed at her hand, pulling her towards him, but Meg refused to be quiet.

'Or maybe she doesn't realise the pressure you're under at work. Or is it that she's too wrapped up in the children and doesn't pay you enough attention?' Tears were coursing down her cheeks—choked, angry tears. She was utterly unable to believe it was all happening to her again. 'I suppose Carla couldn't make it tonight so you thought I'd do to pass the evening! My God, why don't I ever learn?'

'She's dead.' He loosened his hand and Meg's arm fell to her side as the words hit home. 'Lucy's dead.'

He crossed the forecourt to pay.

Mortified, all she could do was stand there—stand there and watch him through the glass, going through the motions, nodding at the checkout girl. Every eye was watching, waiting for the next instalment.

'I'm sorry,' was all she could manage as, grim-faced, he walked back towards her.

'Get in the car. I think we've provided enough entertainment for one night.'

He didn't say anything, not a single word as he shot out of the garage, while Meg sat silent next to him.

'It's left here,' she muttered as they approached the exit for her flat. Ignoring her, he carried on, and Meg sank back in the seat. 'I didn't know.'

Flynn glanced over, then looked back to the road ahead. 'That's your fault; you didn't give me a chance to tell you.'

'I know,' she admitted. 'Where are we going?'

'Here.' Indicating, he pushed a button, and Meg watched as the garage door of a townhouse opened and they glided in. For a second they sat in silence, before Flynn pulled on the handbrake. 'Come on— we'll talk inside.'

She felt him brace himself as he opened the door, and once inside Meg understood why.

Lucy.

Their wedding photo, almost the same shot he had in his wallet, was the first sight that greeted her. Sitting on the hall table right next to the telephone.

She needed a moment—a moment to collect her thoughts, to calm down and work out just how she could even begin to apologise to him.

'Can I use your bathroom?'

'Sure. It's up the stairs on the left.'

Lucy was there too. Oh, there wasn't the usual paraphernalia that women collected, there wasn't a mass of heated rollers and hair tongs, tampons and moisturisers, but her perfume collection still stood on the shelf, and the picture hanging on the wall was so overtly feminine Meg knew at a glance Flynn hadn't chosen it. And what man would ever put an incense burner on the bathroom ledge?

'I'm sorry,' she said for the second time, coming down the stairs. 'I really am.'

Flynn nodded and handed her a glass of wine. 'The worst part,' he started as Meg took a sip, 'was losing a wife who actually did understand me.'

Meg winced, recognising the hurtful words she had so recently thrown at him.

'I was going to tell you tonight, actually.'

Meg nodded. 'I know that now. Flynn, I shouldn't have jumped in; it's just I had no idea—none at all. You don't seem like...' Her voice trailed off.

'Like a widower?'

Meg nodded. It was such a sad, lonely word, conjuring up images of pain and desolation. Nothing like the vibrant, easygoing man she was beginning to finally know.

'How do you expect me to be?' He didn't wait for an answer. 'Walking around with a permanent air of sadness? Crying into my beer at the local pub every night?'

'No,' Meg said slowly. 'It's just that you seem so

content, so unruffled. You don't look like someone who's had an awful past.'

'But I haven't.' His words confused her and Meg looked up, her mouth falling open but no words coming out. 'I've had a wonderful past, with a very special woman. It ended too soon, far too soon, but we still had a great marriage and shared an amazing journey together. I'm not going to spend the rest of my life being bitter, feeling cheated, when in truth I've been luckier than most.'

He sounded so sure, so confident that Meg almost believed him.

Almost.

'How did she die?'

'A car accident.' He took a large slug of wine. 'A truck driver fell asleep at the wheel; he walked away with a bloody nose. I shouldn't have taken it out on you that morning, and for that I'm sorry. I don't often get worked up about it, but it was all a bit too close to the bone. You're about the same age, and when I heard that you'd fallen asleep...'

'I didn't fall asleep.'

Flynn shrugged. 'It's not important now.'

'I was crying.' She was speaking almost to herself, and Flynn looked up, startled at her words. But Meg just sat there, that morning's events slowly coming back to her, terrified to look up, to move, in case the images evaporated.

'I was crying because a child had died. Jess had tried to talk to me and I'd pushed her away, told her I wasn't upset. But I was. I pretended I was tired.' It was all coming back now, flashing into her mind with painful clarity. 'I'd cut my hand on an ampoule.' Looking down, she saw the thin white scar. 'Look.' He took her hand, running his finger along the pale raised flesh. 'I can remember changing gear. It hurt, and I started crying. The next thing I knew I'd missed the bend and a tree was coming towards me.'

'And then?' He was holding her hand, kneeling on the floor beside her.

'You were there.' Meg laughed through her tears. 'Actually, I think it might have been Ken Holmes, the paramedic.'

Flynn gave a dry laugh. 'Don't ruin the picture.' Then his voice changed, urgency taking over. 'Meg, you can't let it get to you like that.'

His statement surprised her. She had been expecting a lecture, to be told in no uncertain terms how she should have opened up to Jess. Not this. 'Doesn't it get to you?' she asked, bewildered.

Flynn shook his head. 'I don't let it.'

'But it must.' She stared at him, genuinely astounded.

'It's a job Meg. A labour of love, maybe, and painful and heartbreaking sometimes, but at the end of the day it's a job. You do your work to the best of your ability and then you go home. That's how you survive it.'

'I can't just walk away and switch off,' Meg argued. 'It's just not that easy.'

'You have to.' He took a deep breath. 'Meg, you smashed your car. You could have been killed—you nearly were,' he added darkly. 'Do you know how many emergency doctors and nurses go home and uncork a bottle, or down a couple of pills so they can get to sleep?'

'I'm not that bad!' Meg protested.

'No, but hell, Meg, you nearly died!'

'I know.' She was on her feet now. 'But it *was* an accident, Flynn. Don't make it more than that.'

'You can't let it get to you like that.'

Meg nodded. 'Lesson well and truly learnt. Look, Flynn, I've been having a hard time recently. I left my old job because everyone—and I mean every-one—seemed to be discussing my personal life. I had an affair with a married man.'

'Vince?'

Meg nodded. 'I didn't know he was married at the time. When his wife found out so did everyone else, my mother and work colleagues included. It's just been a rough few months; that's probably why I'm not coping as well as I usually do.' She flushed, sud-denly embarrassed. 'Here's me banging on about my-self. It must be ten times worse for you. How do you cope, seeing accidents and everything? It must be agony.'

But Flynn shook his head, refusing to be drawn. 'I just try not to compare.' He was swirling the wine around in his glass. 'I'm over Lucy. I've dealt with it.'

But something in his voice warned Meg he was trying to convince himself more than her. 'What was she like?'

'Lucy?' His face brightened up. 'Funny, happy-go-lucky, smart—take your pick. She was into adventure, always planning the next holiday—bungee-jumping one summer, white water rafting the next. Actually, you remind me a bit of her.'

Meg gave a shaky laugh. 'I hate to shatter your illusion here, Flynn, and I'm touched—thrilled, actually,' she half joked, 'that anyone could ever consider me adventurous. But the most adventurous thing I've ever done is go on the big wheel at the fair. And I only agreed to that because otherwise Kathy wouldn't have been allowed to go on.'

Flynn grinned at her grimace. 'What happened?'

'I screamed so loudly they had to stop it, and then I promptly threw up. Dad had to give me a fireman's lift home. And as for happy-go-lucky.' Meg took a deep breath. 'I'm the least happy-go-lucky person I've ever come across. It's only fair to warn you in advance that this conversation will be analysed, scrutinised and distorted beyond repair. So you see, there's really no comparison.'

Flynn pulled her down beside him; putting down his wine glass, he took her hands. 'I meant funny, smart and beautiful…' He swallowed then, his face achingly close, his full lips so near, so kissable. 'And just a little bit crazy'

'So where to now?' Her voice was trembling. His hand was still wrapped around hers, and when he didn't immediately answer, Meg continued tentatively. 'Now we know each other's dastardly pasts.' She flushed then. 'I didn't mean you and Lucy…'

'I know.' His face was moving nearer, his voice low and seductive, his lips just a whisper away. It only took the tiniest motion to move forward, but

Meg knew as she did it would have monumental consequences.

His lips were cool—that was her first conscious thought—and they tasted of wine—that was her second and last as she lost herself in his touch, moved herself closer, felt his arms wrap around her, tasted the passion as his tongue met hers.

'Where to now?' He repeated her words as she broke away, her lips tingling, burning from the weight of his touch.

'Home,' Meg said softly. 'I think we both need some time.'

'What are you scared of, Meg?'

'You,' she said honestly, but without a trace of malice. 'Myself, even. Take your pick.'

'Just because I loved Lucy it doesn't mean there isn't room for someone else.'

'I know that,' Meg admitted. 'But...'

'Why does there have to be a but?'

Meg swallowed. 'We've both been hurt.'

'Maybe it's our turn to be happy.'

Oh, she wanted to believe him, wanted to believe it was all that simple. But how could it be? She needed a clear head, needed clarity before she dived into the sea again only to be bitten. She'd been up against sharks before.

'Please, Flynn, it's better this way.'

He closed his eyes and Meg held her breath. She wanted him, wanted him so badly it hurt, and she knew how much he wanted her. But not tonight. Tonight was precious and sweet; tonight they had bridged the gap—found out so much about each other. The last thing she needed was to sense regret in the morning, for either of them.

'I know you're right,' he grumbled. 'But don't ask me to smile as well.'

'I won't. Just call me a cab.'

He didn't, of course. They drove back to her house in amicable silence, his hand resting gently on her leg between gear changes, and when they approached her street he indicated without prompting.

'Just pull in behind the red car there.'

'Which one's yours?'

Meg pointed to the top floor of a small apartment block. 'You see the balcony with all the Buddhas, statues and wind chimes?'

He gave her a slightly startled look before nodding.

'Well, mine's the one next to it.'

Flynn laughed. 'Thank heavens for that. I don't think I could stretch to the lotus position.'

It was a joke, a tiny insignificant joke, but in Meg's present state of mind even the surf report on the radio seemed to have massive sexual connotations.

'Do you want to come in for a coffee?' Her steely resolve was melting like molten lava now.

'I do,' he said slowly. 'But I'd better not.'

It was what she had wanted him to say, and yet opening the car door and peeling herself out of the seat beside him took an unimaginable effort.

'Meg?'

She turned and lowered her head into the car through the open door, the streetlight illuminating her fluffy curls, her eyes shadowed so he couldn't read her expression.

'Shall I pick you up on Saturday? We could go together.'

'I'd like that, but...'

In the darkness he couldn't see her features, but Flynn just knew that she was nervously chewing her lip. The endearing image brought a smile to his face. 'But what?'

'If we arrive together...' Meg hesitated. How could she explain this without sounding as if she was fishing? How could she ever expect him to understand the strange unwritten rules of her family? 'If we arrive together, my mum will expect...she'll think...' Meg was practically stammering now, and Flynn put her out of her misery and finished her sentence for her.

'She'll think we're an item?'

Her blush was so deep that even if he couldn't see it Meg was sure he must at least be able to feel the heat radiating from her. 'Something like that,' she mumbled. 'Mum doesn't know the meaning of the words "casual date".'

'Would it help make up your mind if I told you that there's nothing casual about the way I'm feeling?'

Nervous but pleased, Meg nodded as Flynn continued. 'Would you believe me if I told you that nothing your mum's going to be thinking hasn't already crossed my mind?'

She did believe him. After all, the last few weeks all she had thought about was Flynn. However reluctant, however suppressed, her mind had been only on him, and now he was telling her he had felt it too.

'So.' He cleared his throat. 'Am I coming to get you or not?'

Suddenly, her reasons for holding on to her heart seemed woefully inadequate; so she might live to regret it, might rue the day she succumbed to his charms, but nothing would ever compare to the regret she would feel if she turned and walked away now. 'Yes, please.' She hesitated for a moment, longing to ask him again to join her, but knowing if she did this time he would say yes. 'I'd best get inside.'

He nodded as she closed the car door, then sat and watched as she walked up the driveway. Only when he saw the light on the top floor flick on did Flynn start the engine and drive slowly home.

The house, always silent, always empty, now had a slightly different feel—the lingering scent of Meg's perfume, the two glasses side by side on the coffee table. It was the first time in two years Flynn actually felt he'd come home.

CHAPTER SIX

'WHAT did Mum say?' Meg asked nervously as Kathy breezed in.

'Oh, she thinks you're covering for me and I'm off for a midnight rendezvous with Jake. The fact she caught me swiping a bottle of cream liqueur didn't help much.' Producing a bottle from under her flimsy cardigan, she grinned. 'I thought it might loosen your tongue a bit. I'm warning you, Meg. I want *all* the details. Don't leave a single thing out.'

'You're here to fill me in, Kathy, not the other way around.' Meg grinned.

'We've got all night. Now, come on, Sis, I need food.'

They had to make do with toast, but there was something strangely therapeutic about a pile of warm buttered toast and a glass of ice-cold liqueur.

'Why didn't you tell me he was widowed?' Meg started.

'I did. I've often spoken about Jake's friend. You probably weren't listening, as usual.'

She had a point. The minute Jake appeared in a conversation Meg had more often than not changed the subject or simply switched off.

'Though I haven't brought him up recently,' Kathy admitted.

'Why?'

'You said you didn't want baggage, remember? And, as much as Flynn might deny it, he comes with a pretty big load.'

'Lucy?'

Kathy nodded.

'Did you ever meet her?'

'No, she died a couple of months before I met Jake. It's actually how we first became close. He was having a tough time with his friend, and I guess I provided a pretty good sounding board. I'd just had my last operation so my physio sessions were pretty long. Sometimes Jake would be tired, or a bit flat, and you know how nosey I am—I just sort of dragged it out of him.'

'Like what? Was Flynn really upset?'

To Meg's utter revulsion Kathy dunked her toast in her drink. Normally Meg would have scolded her, but not this time. She wanted to hear what Kathy was about to say next. 'The opposite. Flynn just accepted it there and then. Told Jake how lucky he was to have had her for so long, how the last thing Lucy would want was for him to mourn her.'

'So why was Jake worried?'

'Come on, Meg, they'd been so close, so happy. No one deals with death that easily. Anyway, next thing he threw in his job in Emergency—said he was going to make Lucy's death count and go into research to find out more about the "Golden Hour". What is that, by the way?'

'The hour after an accident,' Meg answered automatically, but her mind was on Flynn. 'Depending upon the treatment the patient receives then, it dramatically affects their chance of survival.'

'Well, whatever it is, Jake was really worried about him. For the first six months we went out I think Jake spent more time with Flynn than me, sure that each night was going to be the night that Flynn would actually crack, show a bit of emotion.'

'But he didn't?'

Kathy shook her head. 'That's just the problem—he never has.'

'But he seems so together, so laid-back,' Meg mused. 'Maybe he just deals with things privately. Not everyone wears their heart on their sleeve. And as to Flynn going into research—well, I can understand that, see why he might want to do something pro-active; his wife died in an accident, which is his speciality after all.'

Kathy didn't answer for a moment. 'It's worse than that, Meg. Flynn was on the Mobile Accident Unit that went out to her.'

'No!' Unimaginable scenes flashed through Meg's mind; her attempts to justify Flynn's laid-back attitude were dashed in that instant. Every fatal accident she'd been out to had left its mark, but to have actually known one of the victims, to have loved them? The pain Flynn must have experienced, the sheer hell he must have been through was impossible to fathom.

'Apparently he recognised the car as soon as they pulled up at the accident, but Flynn didn't tell the paramedics it was Lucy involved. I guess he knew they'd make him stay back.'

'Was she...' Meg swallowed. 'Was she already dead?'

Kathy shook her head and her eyes filled with tears. 'No. But her injuries were so appalling that they knew within moments of freeing her she'd be dead. Flynn sat there with her in the car, held her hand and talked to her…' Kathy stopped as Meg noisily blew her nose.

'He told her he loved her, how happy she'd made him, that sort of thing.'

'Did Flynn tell Jake that?'

Again Kathy shook her head. 'Flynn never spoke about it. Jake got it all from Ken, one of the paramedics.'

'How does he do it?' Meg asked. 'How did he go through all that and still manage to come back to Emergency?'

'I honestly don't know. The job at Bayside Hospital came up and apparently Flynn jumped at it. Jake was worried what might happen if there was a fatal car accident, he even confronted him about it, but Flynn was his usual laid-back self. "Come on, Jake, stop worrying. I'll be fine. And anyway, it might be months till I'm called out."'

'And look what happened,' Meg said slowly. 'Half an hour into his first shift and I go and wrap my car around a tree.'

'Go gently, Meg.' Kathy's voice had an ominous note to it. 'For all Flynn's easygoing, fun-loving attitude, you're the first person he's asked out since Lucy. I know you've been hurt, but if it's a temporary fix you're after then steer clear.'

'I thought you were on my side, here,' Meg interrupted.

'I am,' Kathy said. 'I'm just warning you to think twice before you jump in. There's a lot of pain there. I know you think you're over Vince…'

'I *am* over him.'

'Good.'

But Kathy's lack of conviction rattled Meg. 'He's married, Kathy—as if I could even think of going out with him again.'

'I know. Look, Meg, Flynn's one of the nicest guys I know. He's been to hell and back and has somehow managed to come out intact. He's kind, funny—a bit opinionated, mind,' Kathy added, rolling her eyes. 'There's nothing I'd like more than to see the two of you together…'

'But? Come on, Kathy, I assume there is one.'

'But there's nothing I'd hate more than being around if it ended. And before you jump in and tell me you're not going to hurt him that's not all I'm worried about, Meg. I'm worried that Flynn might not be as over Lucy as he lets on.' Looking at Meg's pale face, Kathy moved over on the sofa and gave her sister a hug. 'I'm probably just being over-dramatic—you know me, anything for a bit of scandal.' She was trying to lighten the mood, but her words had only echoed the nagging voice that Meg had been trying to ignore.

'Now, we've spoken about you long enough—it must be my turn now.' Rummaging in her bag Kathy pulled out a bridal magazine, happily ignoring Meg's groan of dismay. 'I need help with the cake…'

*   *   *

Proud was the best way Meg could describe her feeling as she walked into the party with Flynn on her arm. Proud of her sister, who looked flushed and radiant in a red, crushed velvet dress sweeping the floor, with her blonde hair framing her elfin face. Proud that Kathy had defied all the odds and had made it in the world. And proud of herself too. How could she be otherwise with Flynn on her arm, recalling the tender kiss they had shared when he had picked her up, a teasing taste of what was to come?

And when Jake stood up and spoke to the assembled guests, told everyone how honoured he felt to be betrothed to Kathy, Meg felt her eyes fill with tears. She watched the sheer love in his eyes when he spoke about his fiancée.

'Hey, what are you getting all choked up about?' Flynn whispered as he stood beside her. 'This is supposed to be a happy occasion.'

'I am happy. I'm really happy for them. That's the problem: I feel really bad about the things I said about Jake. It's just…'

'Come on.' Taking her arm, Flynn led her outside. The manicured gardens were beautiful and he led her to a wrought-iron bench, the sound of a fountain a soothing backdrop.

'You had every right to be cautious,' Flynn said once they were both sitting down. 'And I had no right to judge you without knowing all the facts.' He stared at the water for a while before continuing. 'Kathy's pretty good at playing things down, isn't she?'

Meg managed a watery smile. 'That's one way of putting it.'

'From the way she described things to me it sounded as if her limp was never much worse than now. It was a lot worse, wasn't it?' He didn't wait for her to answer. 'I'm not asking you to break any confidences; I already know. I asked Jake about it.'

'Why?'

'Because I wanted to understand.' Those beautiful grey eyes were staring right at her now, and there was nothing she could do but stare back. 'I wanted to know about you, and Kathy's a big part of you.'

'She was pretty bad,' Meg admitted.

'And it must have been hard on you.'

Meg shook her head. 'What have I got to complain about?'

'That sounds to me like your mother talking.'

Meg blinked, startled by his insight. 'She feels guilty, though there's no reason why she should…'

'She's her mother. And sometimes, when you're scared or guilty, it's easier to be angry. I know—I've been there.'

Meg didn't say anything; she knew the conversation was turning to Lucy, and that she needed to hear this if ever she was truly going to know the real Flynn.

'When Lucy died, I got angry. Not just at the driver who caused it; that would have been too simple. I ranted at the paramedics—sure if they'd got there sooner, instigated treatment, called for medical back-up earlier, somehow she might have lived. Hell, I spent eighteen months doing research—as if somehow I could change the outcome, find something that should or could have been done on the day.'

'And did you?'

Flynn's foot was scuffing the ground. 'No. Oh, the research was valuable—there's a couple of things that are done differently in the Golden Hour thanks in part to me—but at the end of the day nothing that would have saved Lucy.' He stopped looking down at his foot, and so did Meg, their eyes lifting to meet. 'Your mum's probably angry, feeling cheated, and it's her way of dealing with it—the same way you deal with it by vetting anyone that tries to get close to Kathy.'

'It's not just that.' Meg's words surprised even her.

'What, then?'

She shook her head. 'I can't tell you.'

'Yes, you can. Hey, Meg, it's me you're talking to.' Pulling up her chin with his fingers, he forced her to look at him, and though she had only known him the shortest time, though in some ways they were just in the infancy of their relationship, it was as if he were looking into her very soul. 'You can tell me anything.'

'It's too embarrassing.'

Flynn started to smile, but it was without a trace of mockery. 'Not the old ''three times a bridesmaid'' bit, is it?'

Meg let out the tiniest wail of frustration. 'How did you know? Is that what everyone's thinking?'

'It hadn't even entered my head till now.' Flynn laughed, but seeing her embarrassment he quickly changed it to a cough.

'Stop it.' Meg brushed his hand away, but despite herself she could feel a smile creeping on her grumbling lips. 'It's not how I feel, I just know that's what all my aunts are thinking—Mum too, probably. Kathy's not even twenty and she's got it all sorted, and here's old Meg.'

Flynn roared with laughter then and didn't even try to hide it. 'Old Meg! God, just how old are you?'

'Twenty-eight,' Meg muttered.

'Thank heavens for that! I thought you were about to tell me you were in your late forties with a brilliant plastic surgeon. Come on, Meg, you're hardly going to be on a Zimmer frame when you walk up the aisle.'

'I know all that,' Meg wailed. 'I don't even particularly want to get married. It's just what everyone's thinking. I'll be trailing up the aisle behind Kathy and they'll all be whispering into their hymn books about Vince, and how all I can land is someone else's husband.'

'You scarlet woman.'

Her smile was starting to spread, 'You don't think I'm terrible?'

'No,' he replied honestly. 'But that doesn't mean I wouldn't like to get my hands on this Vic.'

'Vince,' Meg corrected. 'Or ''bloody Vince'', as Kathy and I call him.'

'That's much better,' Flynn agreed. 'And no one thinks you're a washed-up old maid. You're just a beautiful *young* woman with a very bruised ego.'

'Who's had too much champagne.'

Flynn shrugged. 'It's a party—your sister's engagement. If you can't have a glass or three and get a bit emotional, then what fun is there in life?'

Meg shrugged. 'I was wrong about Jake; I can see that now.'

'He adores her,' Flynn said assuredly. 'And to prove it I'm going to tell you something that must never go further, no matter what happens to us.'

Us. That single word had the most delicious ring to it, and Meg found herself hanging on to it, dwelling on its implications as Flynn continued.

'Jake hates working in Emergency.'

'Jake?' Meg dragged herself back to the conversation. 'But I thought he loved being a physio.'

'He does.' Flynn nodded. 'He loves rehab—even back in uni it was all he wanted to do. And then he met Kathy. Ten years younger and with a mother like a lioness with a cub.'

A smile was tugging at the corner of her lips. 'Is that a polite term for a battleaxe?'

'It's anything you want it to be. He asked me what to do. Technically he wasn't doing anything wrong in asking her out, and I said the same to Jake as I did to you—he wasn't her doctor. But Jake knew what people might say, and he just didn't want Kathy to be put through the mill any more than she already had been. He applied for the Emergency position before he even asked her out.'

'He did that for Kathy?'

Flynn nodded. 'In a heartbeat. Jake hates handing out crutches and, as nice as he might have been to you, advising people how to cough isn't what he wants to be doing. But he grins and bears it.'

'For Kathy.'

'Pretty nice love story, huh?'

Meg nodded, shocked by what Flynn had told her, yet pleased—so pleased for Kathy.

'You know what you should do?' When Meg looked at him, bemused, he carried on talking. 'Go back in there and congratulate them—both of them— for finding each other; they'll know you mean it now.'

Meg nodded; Flynn was right. But as she went to stand he pulled her back.

'Hey, not so quick.' Wrapping his arms around her, he moved her closer towards him. 'There's something that needs to be taken care of first.'

'What?' Her mind was with Kathy and Jake, and putting right a hundred wrongs, but as she saw his face moving towards her everything bar the moment flew out of her mind like petals in the wind.

'This,' Flynn muttered, his breath warm on her cheek, the solid strength of him drawing her closer. Their lips met, tremulous yet certain, the cool shiver of his tongue against hers, their breath mingling in delicious union. A kiss full of depth and desire and a delicious glimpse of what was surely to come…

'Megan.' Her mother's accent was unmistakable.

They broke apart, laughing like naughty school-children as they hastily arranged their clothes before Mary appeared in view.

'It's Megan when she's annoyed,' Meg explained. 'Which is quite a lot recently.'

'Talk about timing,' Flynn muttered, but Meg just laughed as Mary bore down on them, her face flushed from her one glass of champagne.

'Just what exactly are you doing out here, Megan?'

She cast a disapproving look at Flynn, who was wearing a rather flattering shade of crimson lipstick.

'Where do I know you from, young man?'

Flynn coughed, and Meg was amazed to see this strong confident man for once actually lost for a flippant reply. 'The hospital. I'm the doctor who spoke to you when Meg had her accident.'

But Mary O'Sullivan had dealt with too many doctors in her time to be impressed or intimidated by a medical degree.

'Well, then, can I safely assume you've had a good education, and therefore you know that it's bad manners to leave during the speeches?'

Meg smothered a grin as her mother's steely expression turned to her. 'And as for you, young lady, you haven't even said hello to your aunty Morag.' Marching on ahead, she turned briefly. 'Try and remember to ask about her gall bladder.'

Following subserviently, Meg nudged Flynn, who absolutely refused to catch her eye. 'A lioness, remember?' Meg whispered.

'Maybe,' Flynn said glumly. 'But I'm the one holding her cub.'

The party was in full swing when they returned. With the speeches safely over, everyone in the packed hall was intent on having a good time.

'Flynn!' Kathy screeched as they entered. 'Meg! Mum has been looking everywhere for you.'

'She found us,' Flynn said dryly, which Kathy seemed to find hilarious.

'What's so funny?' Jake came over, handing Kathy a fresh glass of champagne.

'Mum just caught these two outside.'

'So?' He looked over at the two blushing faces. 'Oh,' he said, and started to laugh. 'Thank God for that. It might take the pressure off me a bit.'

And that was that. As effortlessly and as easily as breathing it seemed to be accepted that Flynn and Meg were a couple, and as Flynn dived on a passing waiter carrying trays Meg knew the time had come to let Kathy and Jake know that, at last, she recognised them as one.

'I just wanted to say congratulations, and how happy I am for you both,' she said with feeling as Flynn slipped a supportive hand in hers. 'You're lucky to have each other.'

'You really mean it?' Kathy asked, her face suddenly serious, as if Meg's opinion really mattered.

'I really mean it.' With a slightly unsteady hand Meg accepted the glass of champagne Flynn handed her. 'To both of you.'

'I'll drink to that.'

'While we're all being soppy and emotional, Jake's got something to ask you, Flynn. Haven't you?' Kathy prompted, nudging Jake none too gently in the ribs.

'I have.' He cleared his throat. 'I was wondering—I mean, we were wondering if you'd be my best man?'

The glass that was on the way to his lips suddenly paused, and with a flash of pain Meg knew what Flynn was thinking; they all did. Suddenly the foursome were quiet, knowing how poignant this must be for him, how he must be remembering asking Jake to do the same for him.

For him and Lucy.

'I'd be honoured,' he said quietly, and Meg felt his hand tighten on hers. But even as she returned the small gesture, even as she offered what small support she could, the moment was over, and suddenly it was all slapping backs and hugs and handshakes, all smiles and laughter, toasting the future.

Lucy was Flynn's past, Meg realised, and as much as she might want to share his pain, lighten his load, Flynn wasn't letting anyone in.

'Did you remember to find out about your aunty Morag's gall bladder?' Giggling, immoderately they half fell into her flat.

'Find out!' Meg exclaimed. 'In glorious Technicolour detail! I swear they did it without an anaesthetic the way she went on about it. Can you believe she had the stones in a jar in her handbag?'

Pouring what was left of the cream liqueur Kathy had brought over into two glasses, Meg handed Flynn one.

'And do you think your mother bought our story about sharing a taxi?'

'Not for a second,' Meg replied happily. 'Flynn, I'm old enough to look after myself. I left home eight years ago.'

'I know.' He winced. 'God, she could cut you with a look, your mother.'

Meg laughed, but the laugh faded in a second as she heard what Flynn had to say.

'Maybe I should just be done with it and make an honest woman of you.'

'Flynn?' Meg wasn't sure she had heard right.

'I'm serious, Meg.'

So was she. Incredible as his words were, as much as they had taken her completely by surprise, it was as clear to Meg as crystal that she loved him. 'We hardly know each other.'

'I know that I love you.' He put down his glass and crossed the room. 'Don't ask me to tell you when it happened, because I can't be sure. But looking down at you in resus that morning, yours eyes like a wary kitten, bits of glass strewn through your hair, I wanted to pick you up and take you home. If there's such a thing as love at first sight then it happened to me.'

He ran a finger along her cheek. 'Meg, I never thought I'd be saying this again, but being with you just feels so right.'

'I know it does—but marriage?' She looked up at him. 'Flynn, we haven't even slept together.'

He gave a low, throaty laugh, his tongue tracing the length of her neck, making her toes curl as he nuzzled deeper. 'We can soon put that right.'

One hand was stealing along her waist, searching fingers locating her zip and sliding it down as his warm hand slid inside. With a low moan she felt his hand on the soft mound of her breast, his finger and thumb massaging her nipple. His other hand was brushing her strappy dress down over her shoulders and, moving back slightly, he watched with unmasked admiration as it fluttered to the floor. His tie, already undone, was easily removed, and with almost indecent haste they both attacked his shirt. The need to feel him naked against her was an instinct as natural as breathing. The heavy buckle of his trousers and the tiny silver zip were teasing obstacles for her long nails. Tugging at his trousers, she ran her hand along the solid dusky-haired thighs, the taut, muscular buttocks.

There was nothing now to stop them—no physical obstacle anyway. Just one big question that Meg needed the answer to.

'Are you sure?'

He nodded, the same affirmative nod she had grown so used to, but it had bigger ramifications now. 'Are you?'

Oh, she was sure. Never had she been more so. 'I don't want you to regret...'

'Shh.' Pulling her up, he held her close for a moment. She could hear his heart pounding in his chest, and his fingers were lost in her long dark curls as she closed her eyes and let his words wash over her, soothe yet simultaneously excite her. 'I know how I feel, Meg, and I know how you make me feel. And as long as it's right for you then there's nothing for either of us to regret.' He wrapped his arms tighter around her, pulled her closer if that was possible. 'Is it, Meg? Is it right for you too?'

She nodded into his chest, salty tears of love and joy slipping down her cheeks, moistening his glistening skin beneath her. He laid her down on the floor gently, slowly. Each kiss, each touch, was measured, calculated to bring her to the very edge of reason, the very edge of oblivion. He parted her soft thighs, his fingers tracing the yielding flesh of her womanhood until she groaned for mercy, quivering with desire, almost begging him to enter her welcoming warmth. As he entered her a strangled gasp was forced from her lips, muffled by the weight of his kiss. Then her hips were rising to meet his, grinding in unison, pulling him deeper. He was taking her further than she had ever been in her life, the throbbing intensity of her sweet surrender causing her to cry out his name.

She knew she shouldn't compare—Vince and Flynn were two different entities entirely. And in truth there was no comparison. The exquisite tenderness of Flynn's lovemaking, the adoration in his eyes, should have washed away all the pain of her past. But when Flynn scooped her up in his arms and carried her to the bedroom, gently laying her down and pulling the sheet over her, she felt a surge of panic as he smiled down at her and moved for the door. This was the point when Vince had left. When he'd suddenly remembered an early client, or the car service, when he had kissed her goodbye and said that he'd ring her in the morning.

'Where are you going?' Her voice was tentative, the tiniest note of panic creeping in, and Flynn turned with a quizzical look in his eyes.

'To get some water. Do you want some?'

Relief washed over her. 'Please.'

'Where did you think I was going?' He stood there,

naked and gorgeous. Evading the question, attempting a diversion, Meg stretched seductively on the bed.

But he didn't respond and, looking up, she could see the hurt in his eyes.

'Meg, where did you think I was going?' His voice was slightly louder, more insistent.

'Home,' she admitted finally.

'You think I'd just get up and leave? We just made love, for heaven's sake. Didn't anything I said count?'

Meg rolled on her side, facing the wall. Anything other than see the pained look in his eyes. 'Of course it did.'

'Then why did you think I was going home?'

'Just leave it, Flynn. Please,' she added. But Flynn was having none of it. In two short steps he crossed the room. Sitting on the bed, he raked his fingers through his hair, hardly making a mark in his jet black hair.

'I'm not leaving it, Meg. I went to get a glass of water and you—'

'I made a mistake,' she interrupted. 'Vince—'

It was Flynn that interrupted now, his voice angry, trembling with fury, but Meg knew that it wasn't aimed at her.

'I'm not Vince. Don't ever compare me to him.' His eyes flashed to her and in a second the anger evaporated. Seeing her lying there on the bed, confused, he felt his heart melt. 'I'd never hurt you, Meg. Don't let that excuse for a man ruin it for us.'

'He won't,' she said, her voice trembling. 'He won't,' she said again with more conviction.

He pulled her into his arms, burying his face in her

hair, breathing in her sweet perfumed scent and feeling her fragile and vulnerable beneath his touch. Nothing else but that moment mattered. All he wanted to do was love her, adore her, and all she wanted was him.

Their lovemaking was slower this time, gentler, but the passion, the breathtaking rollercoaster ride of discovering each other, was just as enthralling. And afterwards, as they lay spent in each other's arms, there was no shame in her tears, no turning away and pretending to sleep. Just the gentle peace of acceptance, the utter joy of a new love born.

CHAPTER SEVEN

IT SHOULD have been perfect.

It almost was.

Meg awoke slowly, lying on her stomach, feeling the heavy weight of his leg over her, an arm draped over her back and the soft kiss of his breath on her shoulder. Wriggling slightly, she turned her head, watching Flynn sleep. Watching the sun on his face, the full sensual mouth, the dark hair, his eyelashes short jet spikes, and she waited.

Waited for the pang of guilt, the shame of the morning after, the desire to pull the sheet over her head and groan with embarrassment.

It didn't come.

Instead Meg realised she was actually smiling. Smiling as she watched him wake—the way his eyes screwed up and his lips curled, the restless movements of a body coming out of a deep long sleep. One lazy eye opened, immediately closing as a shaft of sun hit it.

'Morning.' Meg grinned.

He ran a lazy hand over her bottom and despite his grumbling as he awoke Meg knew he was delighted to feel her there from the way he luxuriously touched her. 'Is it morning already?'

'Has been for ages.'

120

He ran a tongue over his lips. 'I shouldn't have had that liqueur.'

Meg laughed. 'Tell me about it! Do you want some coffee?'

He nodded gratefully. 'And a gallon of water.'

Slipping on a robe, Meg padded out to the kitchen. It was only when she was alone, watching the water spurt through the filter machine, that the demons crept in. What if he thought less of her? What if he was lying there across the hall right this minute regretting every moment? What if that dig about drinking a liqueur was his way of saying that he'd never have slept with her if he hadn't had too much too drink?

Stop it.

Pulling the ice tray out of the fridge, she broke some on the bench and filled a long glass. His intentions had been clear long before they had even arrived back at her flat. He had told her he loved her, practically proposed to her! Meg ran the glass under the tap, mentally shaking herself. She was being an idiot.

And anyway, the grin that greeted her when she padded back into the bedroom, balancing a tray and a mountain of Sunday papers, was more than enough to suspend any doubts.

'God, I love Sundays.'

'Me too.'

He read every last piece of the papers, his hand running over her body now and then and taking breaks to kiss her, to laugh with her. Somewhere between the business page and the colour supplement he made love to her all over again, and for a while there Meg thought she had died and gone to heaven.

For a while.

'Hey, sleepy head.' Flynn broke into her postcoital doze.

Sitting on the bed, his unkempt hair and the dark stubble on his chin emphasizing the crumpled white shirt of his dinner suit, Meg thought she had never seen a man more beautiful.

'I have to go.' He watched her force a smile, attempt to mask the disappointment in her eyes.

'Sure.'

'There's a few things I need to take care of.'

Meg glanced at the bedside clock; it was two p.m. after all. 'Okay.' She hesitated a moment before continuing, not sure if she was pushing things too hard. 'I'm on a late tomorrow. Will I see you?'

'I certainly hope so.' He picked up her hair and gently moved it off her face. 'But do we have to wait until tomorrow?'

Hope surged in her and Meg's smile finally caught up with her eyes.

'Do you want to come over to mine tonight? I'll ring for a takeaway.' He was pleating the sheet, his eyes not quite meeting hers, and Meg realised he was nervous too. 'You could bring your uniform—if you want to, that is?'

She did want to; there was nothing Meg wanted more. And this time when he got up to go there was nothing playing on her mind, nothing but all the thrill and promise tonight held.

He hadn't left her much hot water—Meg's tiny flat wasn't exactly designed for two—but it didn't stop her singing or rubbing conditioner into every strand of her hair and body oil into every crevice of her body. Tonight was going to be perfect. She walked back into the bedroom, surveying the tousled bed and the newspapers littered everywhere, and was hard pushed to wipe the grin off her face as she set about tidying up. The place looked as if a bomb had gone off, and when the phone rang it took a moment to locate it under the pile of her hastily discarded clothes.

'Has he gone?' Kathy's voice was a loud whisper, bubbling with excitement.

'Kathy!' Meg exclaimed indignantly. 'We shared a taxi.'

'You might be able to fool Mum…' Kathy let out a low chuckle. 'Actually, you can't. She was out first thing for Mass, and now she's upstairs doing the Rosary. Praying for your sins, no doubt.'

'Well, there's no need.'

'Not feeling guilty, then?'

'Not a bit,' Meg said firmly.

'Good. Well, hold that thought and I'm on my way.'

Meg's stomach let out a huge rumble, and before Kathy could hang up she called her back. 'Stop at the bakers on Beach Road, would you? Bring some croissants.'

'Hungry, are you?'

'Starving,' Meg admitted without thinking, and Kathy started laughing. 'Just bring the pastries.'

Hanging up, Meg dressed quickly and put on the coffee pot for the second time that day. Just as the jug was filling and the flat was taking on a semblance of normality her doorbell rang loudly, and with a wide grin Meg opened the door.

Her grin didn't last long.

'Vince?' He was the last person on earth Meg had been expecting to see, and the shock was evident in her voice.

'I only just heard. I came as soon as I found out.' He ran a hand through his blond hair—straggly hair, Meg noted. And he looked thinner now, with dark rings under his eyes.

Meg gave him a bemused look. 'What on earth are you talking about?'

'Your accident.'

'But that was ages ago.'

'What you must have been through.' He stared at her with sorrowful eyes. 'And I wasn't there to help.'

'Of course you weren't,' Meg said stiffly. 'You were with your wife. How is she, by the way?'

'Meg don't bring Rhonda into it…'

'She's your wife, Vince. I know you seem to find that little fact rather easy to forget, but I for one can't.'

'Please, Meg.' There was a note of desperation in his voice. 'Can I just come inside?'

Her instinct was to scream no, to slam the door in his face and retreat to the safety of her flat. But what would that solve? A slanging match in the hallway she could do without. 'Just for a moment, then,' Meg mumbled, standing back stiffly to let him in.

'Hell, Meg,' he said once the door was closed and the only sound was Meg's pounding heart. 'I've missed you.' When she didn't respond his voice took on a slightly pleading note. 'Please, Meg, when I heard about the accident…'

'Does your wife know you're here?'

'Meg, just listen, will you…'

She swung around then, her eyes blazing with fury. 'What were you expecting, Vince? That we'd fall into bed? That we'd carry on as before?'

'Of course not,' he spluttered.

'Then what?'

'I just wanted to see for myself that you were okay.'

'Well, you've seen.' She held her hands up and slapped them quickly down to her thighs. 'I'm fine. Now, if you'll excuse me, I'm expecting company.' Undoing the latch, she went to wrench open the door—but his hand got there first.

'Please, Meg.' His hand was over hers, and in a reflex action Meg pulled it away. But not quickly enough. The door flew open at that moment, and as Kathy burst in, her arms full of greasy paper bags, the happy smile on her face died in an instant.

'Oh,' she said her eyes turning questioningly from Vince to Meg. 'The adulterer's here.'

'Kathy.' Meg's voice had a warning ring to it, but Kathy hadn't finished.

'He looks like a duck.' She walked over to the bench and put the bags down as Vince stood there, a muscle pounding in his cheek. 'Walks like a duck.'

'I don't need this from you!' Vince had finally found his voice.

'And quacks like a duck!' Kathy finished triumphantly.

'Vince was just leaving.' Meg flashed Vince a look. 'For good.'

'I am allowed to be concerned,' Vince said from hallway the as Meg finally ushered him out. 'We were together for a long time, and they were good times, Meg. You know that as well as I do.'

Meg closed the door behind Vince. Leaning her head against it, she took a deep cleansing breath before turning to Kathy. She had expected a sympathetic grin, or at the very least a look of understanding, not the suspicious, even hostile stare that was coming from the usually easygoing Kathy.

'What the hell are you doing, Meg?'

'He just turned up out of the blue, honestly,' Meg said somewhat taken aback by the accusing note in Kathy's voice.

'I didn't ask what Vince was up to. I couldn't care less about him and neither should you.'

'I don't.'

'Then what were you doing letting him in?'

Meg shrugged. 'What was I supposed to do? Discuss things in the hall so all the neighbours could hear?'

'You shouldn't have anything to discuss.'

'We don't. Look, Kathy, he just found out about the accident. He was worried.'

'I bet he didn't tell his wife he was dropping by.'

'We were together a long time; he was bound to be concerned,' Meg reasoned, but Kathy was having none of it.

Kathy, happy-go-lucky Kathy, who never got rattled, never, ever got cross, was suddenly on her feet, literally shaking with rage. 'Oh, grow up, Meg. Just grow up, will you?'

'What's that supposed to mean?' Instantly Meg was on the defensive. She had truly done nothing wrong and couldn't believe how Kathy was reacting.

'Exactly that. The best thing that's ever happened to you has just rung Jake. He's asked him to go over—wants to move things on in his life.'

Meg shook her head, bemused, not understanding where Jake came into all this.

Kathy threw up her hands in despair. 'Flynn's sorting out his house—clearing things away. He doesn't want to upset you with constant reminders of Lucy when you come over tonight. And what are you doing? Having a cosy afternoon tea with Vince, that's what!'

'Kathy, will you listen to me?' Meg's quiet deliberate tones were such a stark contrast to Kathy's angry rantings that she actually snapped her mouth closed, her suspicious, angry eyes turning to Meg.

'Vince arrived two minutes before you. I honestly had no idea he was coming.'

'Honestly?'

'Kathy, this is me you're talking to. I'm your sister—have I ever lied to you?'

Kathy sniffed. 'Yes.' Her anger was abating and Meg saw a flash of the old Kathy as a reluctant smile wobbled on her lips. 'You told me you'd taken those books back to the library and I found them under your bed.'

'Seven years ago,' Meg pointed out. 'I meant about anything important.'

Grumbling, Kathy picked a bag off the bench. She selected a pastry for herself first then tossed the rest of the bag to Meg. 'I still had to pay the fine.' Closing her eyes for a second, Kathy let out a little sigh. 'I'm sorry, Meg, I just overreacted—seeing that creep here, knowing the hell he's put you through. I just don't want to see you get hurt again.'

'I'm not going to get hurt,' Meg said resolutely. 'At least not if I've got any say in it.' She took a small bite of her croissant. Funny, but after seeing Vince she suddenly didn't feel so hungry.

'Are you going to tell Flynn?' Kathy asked. 'That Vince was here, I mean.'

Meg swallowed the pastry, it tasted like cardboard. 'I don't know. I've done nothing to be ashamed of, but if what you told me about him clearing out the house is true, I don't think it would be exactly great timing. Are you going to tell Jake?'

Kathy looked at her sister thoughtfully for a moment. 'No,' she said slowly. 'But I'm not covering up for you, Meg, and don't ever expect me to. I just don't think Flynn needs it, today of all days.'

'Meg.' He kissed her warmly and fully, right there on the doorstep. 'I was just about to ring and see where the hell you'd got to.'

Meg looked at her watch. 'I'm not even late.'

Flynn pulled her inside. 'I guess I just missed you.'

The first thing Meg noticed, or rather didn't notice when she stepped inside was his wedding photo. It was still on display, she saw when he led her through to the living room, but on the dresser. His eyes followed hers and she felt his hand tighten around her fingers.

'I can't just put it away.'

'I'd never expect you to.'

He cleared his throat. 'I just didn't want you to be overwhelmed.' He showed her around briefly, depositing her bag on the large double bed, and even though Meg had never been in the bedroom before, a woman's instinct told her that the freshly polished smell and the incredibly clean dressing table were the results of a poignant afternoon. Her instinct was confirmed when she excused herself to the loo.

The picture was still on the wall, but the incense burner was pushed back a bit and the perfume bottles had been moved from the bathroom shelf. Maybe she shouldn't have looked, maybe she was being nosy, but even as she opened the bathroom cabinet Meg knew what she would find. There, nestled amongst the combs, shaving brushes and aftershaves, were Lucy's perfume bottles. Sure, he'd moved things around, tried not to overwhelm her, but she knew that when push had come to shove he simply hadn't been able to do it. Taking a bottle down, Meg sniffed at it for a moment, her eyes welling with tears as she inhaled the heady fragrance. Tears for a young life lost. For all Lucy had lost and for all the pain Flynn had been through.

Oh, Flynn.

All she wanted was for Flynn to be honest—not just with her, but also with himself.

But honesty was a two-way street. Replacing the bottle, Meg took a deep breath, and as she headed down the stairs her mind was whirring. She couldn't start with lies, no matter how white, no matter how small. A lie by omission was still a lie, and it was the one thing she dreaded Flynn doing to her.

He had to know.

He handed her a glass of red wine as soon as she stepped in the kitchen. 'I didn't know how you took your coffee,' he admitted. 'And if you don't like red wine, we might as well call it quits now. Joking,' he added seeing her serious face.

'I know.' She took a sip. 'It's delicious.' She didn't know how to start, wasn't sure that she wanted to. But all Meg knew for certain was that she had to.

As it turned out, Flynn made the opening for her.

'I saw Jake this afternoon. He said Kathy was heading your way. How was she? Still on cloud nine after last night?'

'Not exactly,' Meg muttered, swirling the wine in her glass. 'Flynn, there's something I have to tell you.'

'Sure.' He was staring at her so openly, not a trace of concern on his face. Meg had the same feeling that plagued her when she was about to give a baby an injection. That rotten feeling as they smiled at you, trusting and gorgeous, not remotely aware that you were about to stick a two-inch syringe into their fat dimpled legs.

'Vince came over this afternoon.'

'Vince?' His eyebrows creased for a moment. 'You mean ''bloody Vince''?'

'The very same.'

'Are you all right?'

Meg looked at him, a touch startled by his question. 'I guess so. It was just a shock. I thought it was Kathy when I opened the door, and there he was.' She took a large slug of her wine. 'Apparently he'd heard about my accident—said that he was coming to see how I was doing.'

'A bit late,' Flynn snorted, but the scorn was directed at Vince, not her.

'I know.' She simply couldn't believe how well he was taking it. 'I got rid of him as quickly as I could.'

'And he didn't give you a hard time?'

Meg shook her head.

'Good. So why's Kathy upset?'

Meg was staring at his back now. He was pulling open an overhead cupboard and grabbed a large bag of potato chips, tossing them in a bowl as she tentatively continued.

'I think she thought it was a bit inappropriate.'

'Inappropriate? Has she been taking lessons from your mum?' Flynn laughed, really laughed then, and unbelievably, after all her angst of just a few moments ago, Meg found herself joining in.

'She was just worried you might be upset.'

'Had you rung him the second I'd gone, begged him to come over and jumped into bed with him, *then* I'd be upset.'

'How do you know that I didn't?'

Flynn shrugged. 'If you did, why would you be here?' He came over and, taking her wine glass from her, picked her up and deposited her none too gently on the bench, pushing his groin into hers, Meg found her legs instinctively coiling around him as he quietened her with a deep, slow kiss. 'Meg,' he said, pulling away, cradling her face with his hands. 'You don't have to earn my trust; you've already got it. Now, enough about Vince already,' he whispered. 'Let's think about dinner.' He gestured to the fridge door. 'Pick a menu.'

Never had she seen so many takeaway menus. Indian, Thai, Chinese, Mexican—a cultural melting pot right there on his fridge. 'Or,' he said seductively, 'we could skip the main and head straight for dessert.'

'What is there?' Licking her lips, Meg suddenly realised she was really hungry. Her appetite was eternally whetted, though, when Flynn reached over and pulled open the fridge door. Taking out a can of instant whipped cream, he pulled off the lid with his teeth, shaking the can vigorously as Meg let out a gurgle of excited laughter.

'It's anything you want it to be,' he said in a seductive drawl. 'The possibilities are endless.'

CHAPTER EIGHT

WAKING up next to Flynn was, Meg decided, enough of an incentive to turn her into a morning person. Instead of slamming her hand on the snooze button and burying her head further under the pillow, she lay for a somnolent moment, revelling in the warmth of his body, the bliss of feeling his arm around her, recalling the tender, sweet love they had made.

'Hey, sleepy head.'

Meg opened her eyes, the delicious sight of Flynn better than any dream. 'I wasn't asleep.'

'Fooled me.'

It was the tiny glimpses of domesticity Meg adored, like listening to him in the shower as she prepared breakfast. Not exactly a feast of culinary delights—all Flynn's larder stretched to was bread, some dubious-looking jam and a scraping of butter—but taking it back to bed and sharing it with a newly showered Flynn, Meg might just as well have been eating at a five-star hotel, it tasted so divine.

But the real world was out there, waiting, and as the clock edged past seven Flynn reluctantly got up from the crumpled bed and started to dress. 'I'd better step on it.'

'Can't you be late?'

'Charge Nurse O'Sullivan!' Flynn mimicked Jess's strong Irish accent. 'Is that any example to set the students?' Reverting to his own gorgeous deep voice, he removed the breakfast tray from beside her on the bed. 'I'll see you for your late shift. Don't lift a finger. I reckon you've earned a rest—and anyway the cleaner comes in this morning.'

'You've got a cleaner?'

'Best money I've ever spent.' He laughed. 'She's an old sourpuss, so don't bother with small talk.'

'So why do you keep her on if she's so miserable?'

'She can be as miserable as she likes,' Flynn said glibly, knotting his tie with ease. 'She's brilliant at housework, and it's not as if I see her much. The perfect woman, really.'

He gave a wink to show he was joking before leaning over and kissing her goodbye unhurriedly. She could smell the sharp citrus of his shampoo, the musky undertones of his aftershave, and she thought her insides would melt.

'How am I going to keep my hands off you?' he murmured. Resting back on the pillow, Meg half dozed as he filled up his pockets with pagers, a wallet and the usual collection of pens and loose change. 'Just let the answer-machine get the phone.'

'Mmm,' Meg murmured.

'And, Meg, maybe don't say anything to anyone about us just yet.' Her eyes flicked open as he spoke. 'At work, I mean.'

'I wasn't exactly going to walk in with a megaphone.' Sitting up, Meg wrapped the sheet around her breasts, trying and failing to read the expression on his face. In truth she had already decided the same thing—it was just too early and too soon to be the focus of the hospital gossip columns—but hearing Flynn suddenly so cagey was all too painfully reminiscent of Vince.

'I know you weren't,' Flynn replied reasonably. 'There's just a couple of things going on—I haven't time to go into it now.' He glanced at his watch and grimaced. 'I'm seriously behind already. I'll explain tonight. You do understand, don't you?'

Meg nodded, attempting a bright smile, but she didn't understand. How could she? Hadn't Vince always told her to ring his mobile, not to blab too much about them, only allowed a select few friends to see them together? With the benefit of hindsight it was so easy to see why. To see how easily she had been lied to, to see exactly where she had been a fool.

And it wasn't going to happen again.

It was almost a relief when the front door closed. When she could wipe the fake smile off and attempt to gain control of her jumbled thoughts.

Flynn was nothing like Vince.

Nothing.

She was in his house, for goodness' sake, and she would see him at work. Maybe he wanted to be the one to tell his boss—wanted to let the land lie a while so it didn't sound like a brief fling. Dr Campbell was a stickler for the old school ways, and Flynn might be an independent professional, but he still had to toe the line and be seen to do the right thing.

Meg had almost convinced herself, almost assured herself that she was overreacting, reading far too much into a harmless few words. Flynn loved her— he had told her so, and Meg believed him.

Then the telephone rang.

Even if she'd wanted to answer it she couldn't have as the answer-machine picked it up on the second ring. She lay there smiling as she listened to Flynn's rather flip, short message, but her smile vanished as she heard the young, slightly breathless but completely unmistakable voice of Carla on the line.

'Flynn—only me. Pick up if you're home.' So Carla didn't even need to introduce herself. Meg lay there gripping the sheet with clenched fists as Carla paused before continuing. 'I must've just missed you. No worries, I'll see you at work.' She gave a throaty laugh, then lowered her voice, but despite her apparent casual chatter Meg could hear the note of tension in her voice. 'Hey, Flynn, are we ever going to get around to that meal? I'm off next Saturday and so are you. I've checked your roster, so no excuses.'

The beeping of the machine ended the message, but for Meg the agony had just started.

Carla.

Carla leaning over the bonnet of her car. Carla blushing when she spoke, calling Flynn by his first name. Carla the 'family friend'. Who thought nothing of ringing him at seven-thirty on a Monday morning.

And there, Meg realised with a spasm of pain that defied description, was the reason for Flynn's reluctance to go public.

Her instinct was to ring him, to confront him there and then and ask just what the hell was going on, but Meg knew it was pointless. She had to wait—wait until she had calmed down and give Flynn a chance to explain before she judged him. But at the pit of her stomach Meg had already returned her verdict. The result was a foregone conclusion.

Somehow she got through the morning—showering quickly before dressing and heading for home. Not quickly enough, though, to avoid colliding head on with Flynn's cleaner.

'Oh, good morning,' Meg said nervously as she came down the stairs.

The cleaner looked Meg up and down slowly.

'I'm a friend—a friend of Flynn's.' Well, that was one way of putting it she thought wryly.

With a rather curt nod the woman headed off for the kitchen, leaving Meg standing there with her cheeks flaming. Everything, it seemed, had been turned on its head. From her joyous awakening she had been reduced to feeling like some cheap two-minute fling.

All through the day Meg swung erratically between hope and despair. Hope that the love she had discovered in his arms was as true and good as it had felt, and despair that yet again she had allowed herself to be conned.

Any hope of an early answer or resolution was quickly dashed as she entered the department. Trolleys were everywhere, the waiting room humming, and from the frazzled look of the staff as Meg approached for the hand-over she knew there wouldn't be a chance of grabbing Flynn for a coffee.

He was there, though, in the thick of it, listening to a patient's chest in resus. Standing at the white board, Meg tried to concentrate on the hand-over, but her eyes kept dragging back to Flynn, watching as he even managed to make the unwell-looking patient laugh. He must have felt her watching, sensed the weight of her stare, for he looked up, the laugh turning into a small intimate smile as he stilled for a moment. Meg smiled back, a stiff forced smile, and she saw the question in his eyes, the slight furrowing of his eyebrows.

'All right?' he mouthed, and Meg nodded briefly, glad of the excuse to turn away and concentrate on the hand-over.

'I'll hand over cubicle four here.' Jess's attempt at a whisper was fairly fruitless; she could call cows from the top field at the best of times. 'I don't want her husband to hear. Her name is Sonia Chisolm and she came in with facial bruising—the story was that she caught the side of her face on the top bunk, while she was making the children's beds this morning.' Jess paused for effect, her china blue eyes widening, but Meg didn't rise. She really wasn't up to manufactured drama this afternoon; the facts would do nicely.

'Anyway,' Jess continued when it was obvious her audience wasn't going to play, 'unless she was making the bed at ten last night her story doesn't add up. The bruises are at least twelve hours old.'

'Did you ask her how she got them away from her husband?' Meg said wearily.

'I was just getting to that. The husband had to go to a meeting at work—and I mean had to. It was obvious he didn't want to leave. So I had a bit of a gentle chat while I got her undressed.' Jess missed

Meg rolling her eyes. 'There are bruises everywhere and every colour of the rainbow. Anyway, Flynn had a long talk with her. Apparently this is her second marriage—her first husband did the same to her and she left him, but she's sticking by this one. Apparently he didn't mean it—the usual: pressure at work, if she'd only had the house a bit tidier, the kids in bed—all that type of thing.'

'So what are we doing for her now?'

Jess shrugged dramatically. 'I've offered her a social worker and spoken at length about the women's refuge, the police—even Flynn's tried until he's hoarse. But she's simply not budging. Her husband's back now, and he wants to know when she can go home.'

'What does Flynn say?' It was like getting blood from a stone, getting Jess to wrap up a story when she was on a roll.

'Well, what do you know? He wants to admit her to the obs ward for neuro obs. I've told him that we can't. We haven't got enough staff at the best of times, without using it as a women's refuge. There's no medical reason she should stay and she clearly doesn't want any help.'

'So that's it?' Meg felt a flash of anger. 'We just leave it there?'

'What *can* we do, Meg?'

'We could buy her a bit of time. Arrange a social worker to at least attempt a chat.'

'She doesn't want it,' Jess pointed out. 'And at the end of the day she's a grown woman.'

'So it's her fault?'

'I didn't say that. Nobody deserves to be treated like that, but if she doesn't want to be helped there's not a lot we can do. You can only take the horse to water, Meg.'

'Oh, spare me the proverbs.'

'Are we talking about Sonia Chisholm here?'

Meg deliberately didn't look up as Flynn came over.

'Yes,' Jess replied crisply. 'I was just explaining that we haven't got enough staff on to open up the obs ward this evening. If you want to admit her she'll have to come in under Trauma.'

Flynn pushed Sonia's X-rays onto the viewfinder and searched them without answering.

'You can look all you like, Flynn, there's no fracture.'

Emergency was one of the few places in a hospital where a nurse could get away with challenging a consultant to this extent. Here the nurses were more aggressive and more forthright than on the wards. And with good reason. Huge volumes of patients came through the department and it was a constant juggling game to balance policy with patient care. Technically Jess was right, but Meg had a feeling Flynn was about to pull rank.

'Open up the obs ward,' Meg said, handing the keys to Carla, who was obviously enjoying the power struggle. 'I'll do all the admission notes and you can stay round and watch her.' With a sigh Meg ran her fingers through her long dark curls before daring to look up at the livid face of her colleague. 'Jess, you know as well as I do it will be hours before Trauma come down, and by then he'll have persuaded her to discharge herself.'

'And how are we supposed to cover the obs ward? We're two staff down as it is.'

'Suppose it was a genuine head injury?' Meg asked. 'What would we do then?'

'We'd have to ring the agency,' Jess replied, flustered. 'But this isn't a genuine admission.'

'It doesn't mean she doesn't need our help. Look, Jess, if there's any flak for this I'll take it.'

'Doctor!'

Meg didn't need an introduction to realise that the impatient tones were coming from Mr Chisholm. 'My wife's been here for five hours now. Has anyone reviewed her X-rays?'

'I'm just doing that now, sir.'

There wasn't even the tiniest hint of derision in Flynn's voice; there couldn't be. One hint that the staff thought this more than a simple accident and the discussion would be over there and then, with Sonia the only loser.

'Good, so can she go home now?'

Meg watched as Flynn shrugged slightly. 'Look Mr...er...' He looked down at the casualty card he was holding. Meg could only admire him. No one would have guessed they had only just finished discussing Mr Chisolm. 'I don't want to worry you unduly, but I am a touch concerned.'

'Why?'

'Here.' Flynn pointed to the X-ray. 'There's no visible fracture, but your wife is extremely tender—particularly over the temple, and that can be a dangerous spot.'

'But you just said there's no fracture.'

'That doesn't mean she mightn't run into problems. I feel it would be better to err on the side of caution and admit her overnight.'

Mr Chisholm immediately shook his head. 'Not possible. Look, she'll rest at home—I can get my mother in to keep an eye on her. She's just got a small bump on her head—and I thought the health service was stretched for beds?'

Flynn turned back to the X-rays and scratched his head thoughtfully.

'You're obviously a busy man, and admitting Sonia might cause you some inconvenience, but I'm sure you'll agree that your wife's safety is paramount. There is a question as to the length of her loss of consciousness, so I'm really not happy to send her home just yet. We'll keep her in the obs ward, where the nurses will do her obs hourly, and all being well she'll be ready for discharge in the morning.'

The way Flynn had put it Mr Chisholm really had no choice but to agree. He sucked air in between his teeth, and Meg found she was holding her breath as she awaited his verdict.

'Okay, then. If it's better for Sonia.'

Flynn nodded. 'It is. Now, if you'll excuse me, I'd better get on.' And after briefly shaking Mr Chisholm's hand he casually turned and walked off.

Sonia wore an apologetic, anxious-to-please smile while her husband was present, and Meg noted as she ran through her admission history how Sonia's eyes would constantly dart to her husband's before she answered even the most basic question about herself. It was only when his mother arrived and the crying children were obviously ready for an afternoon sleep that he finally left.

The change in Sonia was dramatic. You could almost feel the tension evaporate from the room when he finally left.

'Okay.' Meg smiled. 'Carla will keep an eye on you now. I'll leave you to get some sleep.'

'Is that it?' Sonia asked, a suspicious note in her voice. 'I thought the second he'd gone there'd be a social worker at the end of the bed.'

Meg looked at her questioningly. 'I thought you didn't want one?'

'I don't.'

Meg nodded. 'Then that's your decision and we respect it. Try and sleep.' Meg knew that pushing Sonia now would only put her on the defensive. It had to be Sonia taking the initiative.

'Thanks for before.' Flynn finally caught up with Meg a few hours later, while she was dressing some ulcers on Elsie, an elderly woman who chatted away happily as Meg set about her work. 'Is Jess still upset with you?'

Meg shrugged. 'She'll get over it.'

'How about you? How are you feeling?'

Meg concentrated on cleaning the ulcers. 'I'm fine. Jess's moods don't bother me.'

'I wasn't talking about Jess.'

Meg knew he wasn't, but a patient's bedside wasn't

the place to say the things she wanted to. It was easier for now to dismiss him.

'I'm fine.'

'When's your coffee break?'

'I doubt I'll be getting one,' she answered honestly, but with a slight edge to her voice.

'I'll catch up with you later, then.' He smiled at the patient, and after hovering just a moment finally left, when it was obvious the conversation was going nowhere.

'Nice-looking man,' Elsie commented when he had gone. 'I bet he has to fight them off.'

Pulling a piece of Tubigrip over her dressing, Meg gave Elsie a tight, non-committal smile, which Elsie happily interpreted. 'My George was a looker—real sharp in his day. The girls swarmed over him.' Accepting Meg's help, the old lady lowered herself from the trolley before straightening herself to all four feet eleven of her tiny frame, a wistful look creeping onto her face. 'Only trouble with George was he didn't try so hard to fight them off.' Pulling a compact out of her handbag, Elsie reddened her lips with a sharply pointed lipstick before turning back to Meg. 'How much do I owe you, my dear?'

'Nothing,' Meg said gently. 'How are you going to get home?'

'On the bus, of course.'

'Would you like me to see if I can arrange a taxi?' Meg offered. 'Those ulcers must be very painful.'

Elsie patted Meg's arm. 'The bus will be fine. Now, my dear, why don't you go and get that coffee?

Surely they can manage without you for five minutes?'

They'd just have to, Meg decided. If she didn't sort things out with Flynn once and for all she was going to explode. The only trouble was, now she'd taken the initiative and told a still fuming Jess she was taking a well-earned break Flynn was nowhere to be found.

She headed off to the staff room for a coffee she neither wanted nor needed, and the vision of Carla and Flynn sitting together on the obs ward talking quietly, the curtains drawn around Sonia's bed, wasn't exactly a sight for sore eyes.

'How,' Meg said in a crisp voice, rather reminiscent of Jess's, 'are you supposed to observe your patient, Carla, if the curtains are closed?'

Carla stood up abruptly, but Flynn just sat there, not even managing to look remotely guilty. 'The social worker's in with her. Flynn was just writing the referral. I thought I might give them a bit of privacy.'

'Oh.' Meg beat back a blush. 'Did Sonia ask for her?'

'Yep.' Flynn signed off the piece of paper he was scribbling on. 'She asked Carla to fetch me, we had a chat, and Sonia seemed pretty adamant. So I paged the social worker, who came more or less straight down. Did you need me for anything else?' he asked Carla, scraping the chair as he stood up. Without waiting for an answer he turned to Meg. 'Can I have a word, Meg, in private?'

'Sure. I was just going on my coffee break.'

Meg had been all set to confront him, but standing

in the deserted staff room she was somewhat taken back when Flynn closed the door and in no uncertain terms turned the tables, his angry voice unfamiliar. 'What's the problem Meg?' Not leaving her time to answer he continued, obviously rattled. 'What am I supposed to have done now?'

'Meaning?'

'Oh, don't play games. You've been avoiding me all afternoon. We made love last night, for heaven's sake. I left you in my bed this morning and everything was fine—more than fine. Something's happened and I want to know what. What am I being hung for this time?'

Meg swallowed, hesitant to tell him, realising how petty her accusation would sound, how stupid she had been to doubt him. 'Nothing. I'm just tired, I guess.'

'So there isn't anything upsetting you?' His eyes were searching her face, his voice almost pleading for an answer.

Meg shook her head and smiled. 'I was trying not to make things too obvious, I guess I must have gone too much the other way.'

'So we're fine?' He put a hand up to her cheek and Meg held it there.

'We're more than fine.'

'You'd tell me—if there was something worrying you, I mean?'

Meg nodded, and as he placed the gentlest of kisses on Meg's lips she regretted doubting him.

'Good. Look, I'm off at six. How about I go home and fix up some dinner?'

'You mean ring for a takeaway?

'A guy's gotta eat.'

'How about you go home and have a sleep and *I* pick up the takeaway?'

Flynn gave a low, pleased groan. 'Keep going— don't stop now. Bed, food, then you—sounds great.'

Meg laughed. 'How about bed, me, then food?'

'Better and better.'

The intercom summoning them both to resus was the only thing that stopped them kissing. Rushing around setting up for the cardiac arrest being brought in, they shared a tiny secret smile, and Meg thanked her lucky stars she hadn't confronted him about Carla. She would talk to him tonight, sensibly and with a level head. Flynn had made it clear he would put up with anything except irrational jealousy.

The house was in darkness as Meg pulled up. A storm had broken and rain lashed her as she scooped up the takeaway. Locking up her car, she wished she had a key to Flynn's home. Not for any proprietary status, just for the delicious thought of slipping in unnoticed, climbing into the warm bed where he slept and waking him in the most intimate of ways...

The doorbell would have to do for now, and as she rang it Meg fully expected a couple of soggy minutes' wait in the pouring rain while Flynn orientated himself and staggered downstairs. She was somewhat taken back when the door opened almost immediately.

'Were you asleep?' Meg asked, stepping inside.

'No.' He took the bags from her and headed off towards the kitchen. 'Just thinking.'

'In the dark?' It was only then Meg realised that he hadn't kissed her hello, that he didn't seem particularly thrilled to see her.

'I had a light on,' Flynn replied in a heavy voice. She couldn't read his expression in the darkness, but there was nothing relaxed about the atmosphere. Flicking on the hall light, he gestured upstairs. 'Come on—I'll show you.'

It was exactly as they had decided—bed then dinner—but Meg knew she wasn't heading upstairs to be ravished, and with a sinking feeling followed him.

'See.' He pushed open the bedroom door and walked in behind her. The room was in darkness, the only light coming from the flashing answer-machine—a tiny red light, indicating trouble. Walking over, he played the message, and Meg stood there not moving as she listened to Carla's voice for the second time.

'Seven thirty-two,' Flynn repeated, his voice imitating the electronic American accent that concluded the message. 'Which no doubt means you were lying in bed listening to it?'

Meg nodded.

'And, unless your pet goldfish died and you wanted to spare me the grief, I'd pretty much put money on it that this message was what was upsetting you when you came to work. You were going on about Carla when you found out about Lucy. All that rubbish about us not being too obvious was a lie.'

Again Meg nodded, standing there frozen as he sat on the edge of the bed, resting his head in his hands with a sigh. Even in the darkness he looked beautiful.

'I can't do this, Meg.' He looked up and a flash of lightning illuminated his face, casting shadows on his high chiselled cheekbones, the darkness of his unshaven jaw, his eyes dark pools of pain.

She took the two steps necessary to cross the room, but the void between them was much wider than that. Putting her hand out, she touched his bare shoulder, felt the slump of his usually taut muscles, sensed the despair in him. 'Flynn, don't.' She felt like crying but held it back. She needed to be rational, calm now. Her insecurity had already done enough damage.

'I can't walk around on eggshells.'

'You won't have to,' Meg pleaded. 'I was just upset. Carla's got a thing about you...'

'That doesn't mean I've got a "thing" about her.' He brushed her hand off his shoulder, and the pain of his dismissal was as unbearable as the anger in his voice.

'Flynn, she rang you at seven-thirty in the morning and asked you out for a meal...'

'I've explained—she's a family friend.'

'Who's nineteen and gorgeous, with a king-size crush on you.'

Flynn shook his head angrily.

'She has,' Meg insisted, but Flynn wasn't shaking his head at her statement, more at her absolute refusal to see the problem.

'So?' Leaping to his feet, he stood there, angry and confrontational. 'She rang me, Meg, she asked me for a meal—not the other way around.' Again he shook his head, a weary sigh coming from his parted lips. 'She's nineteen, for heaven's sake, I'm thirty-four.'

'Hardly a hanging offence,' Meg quipped, her intentions to stay calm evaporating as she leapt to her own defence. 'Your words, Flynn, not mine. Is Carla the reason you wanted to keep quiet about us at work?'

Flynn nodded, but there wasn't a trace of guilt on his face. 'I wanted to talk to you about it, see how I was going to handle it. I know her parents well, and I'm going to have to see her long after her crush has ended. I just wanted to give her the out with her dignity intact.'

'Oh, very noble.'

Flynn snorted. 'The most stupid part of it is I was hoping you'd understand—give me some insight as to how I was going to deal with it. Seems I was wrong on all counts.'

'I would have understood, Flynn. If only you'd told me.'

'That's the crux of it, Meg. What do you expect me to do? Sit with you over the dining room table and run through my life story, just in case something pops up that might be misinterpreted? I can't even get a glass of water without you thinking I'm about to do a bunk.'

'That was a mistake; it happened once.'

'The trouble with you, Meg,' Flynn said slowly, ignoring what she had said, 'is that you're so sure you're going to get hurt. So sure that if you open up and actually let the world in it will end in tears.'

'Looks like I'm right,' she said as a salty unwelcome tear splashed down her cheek. Flynn seemed to wince when he saw the tear, his hand reaching up for a second, then pulling away. Instead he ran the frustrated hand over his face.

'I can't live like that, Meg. I can't be constantly looking over my shoulder, wondering what I've said or done to upset you. Things like this don't go away. The deeper we get, the worse it's going to be. It's better this way.'

'You're probably right.' The calm dignity in her voice surprised even Meg. 'But I think you're being a bit harsh, blaming this all on me.' Walking over to the dressing table, Meg picked up a photo of Lucy. 'Before you say it, no, I'm not jealous of her. And something tells me, Flynn, that you were looking for an excuse to end it. Maybe you're not as over Lucy as you make out.' She placed the picture on the bed beside him; it didn't make a sound as she rested it on the thick duvet. He turned and looked at it for a moment, before sitting back down and staring ahead.

'I know I'm not trusting, Flynn. A year and a half of deceit put paid to that. But I'm working on it. I know I can be jealous, and doubting, but if you really loved me, if you really wanted to, you would understand. We got together too soon. You might not admit it, but we're both on the rebound—we've both been hurt. I'm not comparing my grief and pain to yours— we both know you'd win hands-down.'

'It's not a competition,' Flynn said, his voice a raw whisper.

'I know,' Meg admitted. 'And I'm pretty sure you love me, Flynn. I think you even meant it when you spoke about marriage.'

She watched as he screwed his eyes closed. 'I did mean it, but…'

That horrible three-letter word ended all her dreams, and Meg knew there and then she had lost him. 'Here's the ''but'', Flynn: it was just all too good too soon, and neither of us were really ready. I can see that now.'

'This isn't about Lucy,' he insisted, but the certainty had gone from his voice. 'I'm over her.'

'So you keep saying. You can shuffle her pictures about, move her things and pretend that you've dealt with it, but it can never be that easy, Flynn. Something tells me that you're just as scared and just as mistrusting as me. The only difference is that I don't hide it as well. So, either we be honest with each other and admit our weaknesses and try to work through them, or we walk away. Is that what you want, Flynn?'

Almost imperceptibly his eyes darted to the photograph, then back to Meg's. 'This isn't about Lucy,' he repeated.

'I take it that means you're choosing the latter?'

His slow nod was the final nail in the coffin, and, making for the door, Meg stifled the sob that was welling in her throat, holding onto the door handle when his voice called out to her.

'What are you going to do?'

Hesitantly she turned. He was still sitting there, and Meg fought an irresistible urge to rush over and wrap her arms around him, to cry with him as they held each other, and kiss away the pain they both felt.

'Get on with living. I've got a bit of catching up to do.'

'You'll be all right?' Trust Flynn to ask, to break her heart and then check to see that she would be okay.

'That's not your concern.' But even as she said it Meg knew the bitterness in her voice wouldn't help either of them. 'I'll be fine,' she said gently, her face softening, her voice a touch unsteady but her words heartfelt. She even managed a tremulous smile. 'Swollen eyelids and a cracked nose tomorrow, no doubt, but you can't begrudge me that!'

Flynn tried to smile back. 'I'm sure I'll look the same.'

CHAPTER NINE

BUT he didn't.

It was as if their brief affair had never happened. Not a trace of a blush, not a shadow of pain marred his perfect features. If Meg had been worrying about how she was going to face him, then it had been unnecessary. He set the tone the very next day—jokey, pleasant and utterly normal.

Somehow she limped through seeing Flynn at work. Somehow Meg got up each day, showered and put on her make-up. Hell, on a good day she even managed to share a joke with him—about work, of course. Their private lives were off limits, and neither of them ever crossed that line. And, though she searched for a chink in his armour, the tiniest sign that the demise of their relationship had caused him even a millionth of her own agony, not once did she see it.

Well, what had she expected? Meg asked herself. He had got over the death of his much-loved wife; how could a brief fling with a colleague even begin to compare with that?

But it had been so much more than a brief fling for Meg, so very much more. And, despite her best attempts to put it behind her, to build a bridge and somehow get over it, as Flynn forged ahead in his career, as his colleagues warmed to his affable char-

acter, as the department lifted under his knowledge-
able leadership, the gulf between them widened. Meg,
never the most outgoing in the department, never the
most popular, struggled through each day, the pain
she witnessed in the name of duty only adding to her
grief. And she knew that it was only a matter of time
before the winds of change forced a resolution.

As she arrived for an early shift one day, the dis-
array in the unit for once didn't match Meg's emotions. Finally, after much soul-searching and the best
part of a bottle of red with Kathy, Meg had made a
decision—a big one. Now all she had to do was see
it through.

'What's going on?' Meg asked Heather, the Night
Charge Nurse, who was busily setting up resus. A
couple of the staff were pulling over trolleys to make
up extra beds and the overhead tannoy was crackling
into action, urgently summoning the trauma team to
the department.

'Multi-car pile-up on the Beach Road—two fatalities and five serious injuries. We've just sent our
Mobile Accident Unit out to it.'

Meg rolled her eyes. 'Where do you want me?'

The radio link to the ambulance buzzed then, and
Heather rushed to get it. Meg didn't wait for further
instruction and started to run some Hartmann's solu-
tion through a giving set, simultaneously connecting
an ambu bag to an oxygen outlet as she did so. Five
multi-traumas at one time was enough to stretch even
the biggest of departments.

'One's being directly lifted to the Trauma Centre,'
Heather said as she returned. 'But apparently there's

another pile-up on the Eastern Freeway, so everyone's stretched. Looks like we could get the remaining four. The first is already on the way.'

'We'll cope,' Meg said assuredly. 'The day staff are all arriving now. Have you called Dr Campbell and Flynn?'

Heather nodded as she worked. 'Dr Campbell's on the way, but Flynn was already here with a query epiglottitis. He went out with the Mobile Accident Unit. I felt wrung out when we'd got the child safely intubated and airlifted to the Children's Hospital, and now this! What a night.'

Meg gave a half-laugh. 'It ain't over yet, kid,' she joked, but her heart wasn't in it. Her mind was with Flynn. Out facing his demons. Stuck on the freeway with two fatalities and serious injuries. And the worst part of it, the hardest bit of all, was that it was no longer her place to be there for him. He had made that perfectly clear. 'Looks like we're pretty much set up? What's the ETA?'

'Five minutes for the first,' Heather glanced at her watch. 'Which is up.'

'I'll go and meet the ambulance.'

She stood on the forecourt, watching as Security pulled cars over to clear the hospital entrance, aware of the curious looks of staff who had hung around to see what was arriving. Normally Meg loved this bit. The pit-of-the-stomach thrill of excitement as the sirens neared, the first glimpse of the flashing lights, the slight headiness at an impending drama, showing off a touch, knowing everyone was watching.

But not today.

Today her heart was too heavy and her mind too filled with what Flynn must be suffering to enjoy her work. As she pulled on the shiny silver handle of the ambulance door and saw the paramedics massaging the stilled heart, saw the bloodstained mangled wreck of a life, all she felt in that tiny silent second was sadness. Sadness for the people going to work, setting about their day, and ending up fighting for their lives. Sadness for the relatives who had to sit and drink machine coffee for hours, their world temporarily on hold as they rang around chasing people up, trying to be strong as they awaited their loved one's fate. And sadness for the staff who dealt with it. The staff who, day in and day out, pulled on their uniforms just to pick up the mess of other people's lives. Who bandied about expressions such as 'avoiding burn-out', or 'peer support', when they all knew it caught up with you in the end. You wouldn't be human otherwise.

Climbing in the ambulance, she took over the cardiac massage from Ken, and for just a second they shared a knowing look.

Life was bloody awful sometimes.

But there wasn't time for introspection, not when people's lives depended on you. So Meg ran along with the stretcher, massaging the unlucky woman's chest as they raced through to resus. They lifted her over on Dr Campbell's count and she concentrated on the moment, fought hard to save the life of someone she'd never met, nor probably would again. As the other resus beds filled up with the victims, as other teams attended the wounded, Meg battled along with her team. Pushed through bag after bag of blood, drew up drugs, wrote down the hastily shouted obs, set up equipment and picked it back up off the floor when a doctor threw it across the room in frustration.

And when it was over, as everyone who had worked on the woman had known it would be, Meg sat with the relatives as Dr Campbell delivered the terrible news. The only saving grace was that they could look them in the eyes and say that they'd given it their all—that, though it mightn't help now, somewhere down the track it might comfort them to know that their beautiful wife, mother and daughter had had the best treatment available.

Only sometimes it wasn't enough.

'No good, then?' Ken caught up with Meg as she came out of the interview room.

Meg shook her head. 'She just lost too much blood. The faster we put it in, the faster she lost it.' Looking down, she saw he was holding a patient card. 'Another one?'

'Only me. I cut my arm when we were lifting the last one; it just needs a couple of steri-strips whenever you've got a moment. I know it's been hell.'

Meg peeled back the wad of gauze from Ken's arm. 'I think you need more than a couple of steri-strips.'

'It's no big deal.' Ken was in his fifties; he'd been there and done that too many times to get worked up over a small cut. 'I'd have stuck a plaster on it and forgotten abut it if Flynn hadn't seen it.'

Meg felt her insides flip just at the mention of his name. Focussing on replacing the gauze, trying to keep her voice casual, she popped open a bandage and wrapped the gauze in place. 'How was he? At the accident, I mean.'

'Great. You know Flynn—had everyone organised in two seconds flat and still managed to crack the odd joke...' His voice trailed off and he searched Meg's face questioningly. 'You know, don't you?'

Meg nodded.

'Not many do,' Ken said thoughtfully. 'He doesn't exactly make it public knowledge.'

'So how was he this morning?'

Ken took a deep breath. 'Well, he didn't throw up like he did after we got you out, but if his colour was anything to go by I'd say he wasn't far off.'

'He was sick?' Meg's recollection of her accident was hazy at the best of times, but Ken's words stirred her deeply buried images—waiting for Flynn to come to the ambulance, the concern in Ken's eyes when he'd finally appeared, grey and sweaty. She knew for a fact, then—knew for a fact that her instincts were right. Flynn could scream from the rafters that he was coping, deny the world had hurt him, but the truth, however vehemently opposed, was crystal-clear.

Lucy's death had devastated him.

Meg's jealous insecurity, her crippling self-doubt, might have played a part, but she and Flynn had been finished before they'd even started. Like the poor patient lying in resus, from the moment of impact, the moment their two worlds had collided, the end had been inevitable.

'You know, Meg, I've seem some bloody tragedies in my time. But that day, going out with Flynn and seeing what he went through...' Meg was horrified to see Ken's eyes mist over. 'Well, no one should have to go through what Flynn did. I know it's a different hospital, and a couple of years on, but given what he's been through that guy deserves a medal for what he did this morning.'

But Flynn didn't get a medal. He got a cup of cold coffee. And by the time the last of the motor accident patients had been moved out of resus, and the shelves had been restocked and the floor mopped in preparation for the next unfortunate who needed it, Meg's half-day was almost over.

'Bet you're glad to be finished?' It was the first time they had actually caught up that day, and Meg was writing her notes, trying to remember if it was the left or right elbow she had just examined on a screaming two-year-old.

'That's an understatement. Left,' she added, and Flynn gave her a quizzical look. 'Sorry—there's a query epicondylar fracture for you in cubicle two. I was just trying to remember which arm.'

'Thanks.'

'How are you feeling? I mean, I gather it was pretty messy out there this morning.' They might not be lovers any more, but they were still colleagues. It was only right that she ask.

Flynn took the child's casualty card from her before he answered. 'It wasn't great—but, hey—' he gave a shrug '—that's what we do for a living, Meg.' Picking up his stethoscope, he draped it around his neck and flashed his usual smile. 'Catch you later, then.'

Meg just stood there; suddenly she was tired. Tired

of the stupid game they all played each day; tired of
pretending she was coping. She realised there and
then that the decision she had made was the right one.
Now all she had to do was tell him. 'Just who do you
think you're fooling, Flynn?'

'Don't start that again, Meg.' He held out his
hands, joking to the last. 'See, not the tiniest tremor.'

'Flynn, will you just stop for a moment?'

His smile faded as he heard the serious note in her
voice.

'There's something I have to tell you.'

'Are you worried about the wedding rehearsal? If
you are then there's no need. I won't let on for a
second there's any tension...' His voice trailed off as
Meg shook her head.

'It's not that.'

'So what is it? Tell me.'

The annexe was deserted, but Meg shook her head.
'Not here.'

His office was tiny, more an overgrown cupboard,
really, and the piles of notes and X-rays littering the
chairs and desk only made it appear smaller.

'Before I start, I'm only telling you this because...'
She was struggling to find the words, acutely aware
it was their first time alone since the break-up. 'I just
don't want you to feel responsible. This has nothing
to do with you. I'm only telling you first because
you'll find out soon enough anyway.'

One look at his paling face and Meg realised what
he was thinking—realised what her jumbled attempt
at an explanation must have sounded like.

'I'm not pregnant,' she blurted out. 'God, you didn't think I was pregnant, did you?'

Flynn gave a relieved laugh. 'Well, see it from my side. Six and a half weeks after we make love you're looking like you haven't slept in a while and asking to see me in my office.' He put a hand up to her chin, pulling her eyes up to meet his. But it wasn't the gesture of a lover, more of an affectionate friend. 'We'd have coped if you were, Meg. I'm not that nasty!'

'I never said that you were.' His eyes were doing the strangest things to her, and Meg dragged hers away, knowing she couldn't get through this if she had to look at him as well.

'I'm handing in my notice, Flynn.' Meg was looking at her feet as she spoke.

'No.' The word was instant, decisive. 'No,' he repeated. 'Meg, you don't have to do this. We're fine, no one knows—'

'It isn't because of us,' Meg interrupted.

'Then why?' His fingers were back, forcing her chin up, forcing her to look at him, and suddenly she couldn't bear it. There was nothing friendly about his touch and nor would there ever be. Pushing his hand away, Meg took a deep breath.

'I can't do it any more, Flynn. I've loved Emergency, adored it, but not any more. I'm simply not enjoying it.'

'You're just tired,' Flynn insisted. 'Everyone feels like this sometimes, but it doesn't last for ever. Sooner or later the sparkle comes back and you remember why you're here in the first place.'

'Is that what happened to you?' She saw the shut-
ters come down and immediately regretted her words.
'Sorry, Flynn, that's not any of my business.' She
closed her eyes, searching for the words to articulate
her feelings, trying to explain what she didn't understand herself. 'I'm going to go and lay out a body
now. It should have been done hours ago, but we
didn't have the staff and we didn't have the time.'

'Because you were busy looking after the living,
Meg,' Flynn reasoned. 'I can't believe you want to
throw it all away. You do love it, Meg, you do. When
Debbie had to be rushed to Theatre…'

'She lived, Flynn.'

'And so did three of the motor accident victims that
came in this morning. They lived because of us.
Because people like Ken, the police and the firefighters were on the ball. Because when they arrived here
they had staff who were up to date and trained to their
back teeth. Yes, there's a body, but there are also
three people who are going to go on and have good,
productive lives. Forgive me if I sound conceited
here, Meg, but it's because of people like us.'

'I know that.' She was almost shouting. 'But it isn't
just a body to me, Flynn, and it isn't just a job. I
nearly died because I was so broken up at losing a
child. The emergency line bleeps and I go cold,
Flynn, when I used to get excited. To work here you
have to be an adrenalin junkie, and it's just not me
any more. All I want is to come to work, do my job
and then go home.'

'So what will you do?' She could feel his eyes on
her, yet still she couldn't bring herself to look at him.

'There's a Charge Nurse position being advertised on the surgical day unit.'

'Oh, come on, Meg,' Flynn scoffed. 'Lumps and bumps and circumcisions—you'd be bored stiff in a couple of weeks.'

Meg gave a low, tired sigh. 'Sounds perfect.'

'And there's nothing I can say to make you change your mind?'

Meg shook her head. Tears were threatening now, and the last thing she wanted to do was break down.

'We'll all miss you.'

'I doubt it. Oh, maybe when Jess does the roster, but I don't think I made much of an impression down here.'

'You did on me.' His simple honesty made Meg look up. 'I'm going to miss you.'

'Thanks.'

'Does anyone else know?

Meg nodded. 'Kathy. She's coming over again tonight; she's been really good.'

She turned to go, but there was one question bugging her—one final thing she needed to know. 'Flynn, can I ask you something?'

He was sitting on the desk, his long legs dangling, tapping a pencil on his thigh, and he looked up at the questioning tone in her voice. 'Ask away.'

'Why did you come back? Was it because you missed it so badly, or to prove that you could still do it?'

For an age he didn't speak, the only sound the tapping of the pencil on his thigh, and when finally he answered Meg was almost knocked sideways by the confusion in his voice. 'I don't know, Meg,' he said slowly. 'I really don't know.'

Closing the door, Meg realised it was the first time she had heard Flynn sounding anything other than assured.

Through all the turmoil, all the hell of the past few weeks, her staunchest ally had been Kathy. Kathy— who had warned her, tentatively forecast that it might end up in tears—had never once admonished her or said I told you so. Instead she'd arrived with chocolate or wine, rattled on about the wedding reception, moaned about their mother and, despite organising her wedding, had done everything and anything to be there for her sister.

And now, on the eve of her wedding rehearsal, Kathy had again put everything on hold. Even though Meg and Flynn had been over for weeks now, Kathy wasn't insensitive enough not to realise that the wedding would only serve to ram home her sister's loss, nor that, given the fact that today Meg had said goodbye to eight years of emergency nursing, a well earned post mortem was entirely called for.

'I know I was out of order,' Meg said for the umpteenth time. 'I know I was too needy, too suspicious. But I would have changed.'

Kathy shook her head. 'You didn't need to change, Meg,' she said resolutely. 'You just needed a bit of time to find your feet and get back to the old Meg. You're the least suspicious person I know—at least you were until you found out about Vince. How else would he have managed to fool you for so long otherwise?'

Leaning over, Kathy topped up their glasses. Wine and watching slushy films on Meg's couch was an all too familiar routine at the moment.

'Will you be all right—tomorrow, I mean? I can come round and pick you up if you don't want to arrive on your own.'

'Please.'

Even though she had seen him every day at work, the thought of seeing him at such an intimate occasion, seeing Flynn surrounded by her family, had Meg in a spin. The whole wedding did, actually.

From the church service at one right through till they waved off the happy couple she and Flynn would be together, part of the glossy bridal party, smiling, toasting Kathy and Jake and dancing the mandatory slow dances. Meg closed her eyes. How was she going to do it? How was she supposed to get through this and come out with her pride intact? How could she dance with him and expect to somehow conceal the simple fact that she loved him?

Always would.

'Maybe we should have done that?' Kathy's voice seemed to be coming from far away.

'Done what?'

Kathy gestured to the television, but the film might just as well have been in Chinese for all the attention Meg was paying. 'Elope. Are you even trying to watch it, Meg?'

'No.' Meg admitted. 'I'm having a major panic attack about Saturday. Even the rehearsal tomorrow is sending me into a spin.'

'I feel awful,' Kathy groaned. 'I've honestly tried with Mum.'

Meg knew that to be true. Kathy had done her best with Mary—tried to persuade her to relax the rules, bend the occasion to fit in with the uncomfortable circumstances. But Mary O'Sullivan had waited a long time to see one of her daughters walk down the aisle, and there was no leeway in her newly purchased book of etiquette for the sisters to argue the point. Jake and Kathy would walk through the reception hall to the cheers and toasts of the crowd, followed by the best man and the bridesmaid, and bringing up the rear would be the bridal party's parents. That was what the book said and that was what was going to happen.

And that was only the start.

Meg hesitated, unsure whether or not to ask the question that was bothering her. 'Has Flynn ever said anything to Jake? About me and him, I mean.'

Kathy didn't answer.

'Come on, Kathy, I'm not going to let on to him. Surely you can tell me what he's been saying. I need to know.'

Meg was ready for anything—had braced herself to hear the worst, prepared herself for just about any eventuality, even if it involved a nineteen-year-old called Carla. The only thing she had never anticipated was the stab of pain she would feel when she heard Kathy's hesitant answer.

'He hasn't mentioned it.'

Meg sat there for a moment, digesting the news,

her mind searching for comfort. But there was none.
'Nothing?'

Kathy sat there uneasily as Meg pushed harder.
'You mean he hasn't said a single thing about me?'

'I'm so sorry, Meg.'

She crumpled then, right there in front of Kathy.
She just seemed to disintegrate. Kathy let her cry a
while peeling off tissues and topping up her glass,
before she gave up being the brave one and joined in
too. The sight of Kathy's tears was enough to stop
Meg. 'I'm sorry too. You've got the rehearsal tomorrow and the wedding on Saturday. You don't need
this right now.'

'Don't worry about me,' Kathy said, giving Meg a
big hug. 'You know how much I love a drama. If I
can cry at films why not real life? Anyway, just because he hasn't spoken to Jake it doesn't mean he
doesn't care. It's what he did with Lucy—just carried
on like nothing had happened.'

'But something did happen, Kathy. Something big
and beautiful. We fell in love and he's just walked
away without a second glance.'

'That's Flynn for you.' Picking up her glass, Kathy
turned back to the film. 'That's Flynn.'

The rest of the film they spent munching chocolate,
with one sister or the other occasionally coming up
with a scheme that might just save the day.

'You could always sprain an ankle,' Kathy suggested as the final credits rolled. 'At least then you
wouldn't have to dance with him.'

Meg snorted. 'Mum would just make him shuffle

me around in a wheelchair. I can't get out of it, Kathy. You know what Mum's like.'

'You don't think she's got ulterior motives?' Kathy said suddenly. 'She's not trying to play matchmaker, is she?'

Meg gave a scornful laugh. 'Who? Mum? She hasn't got a romantic bone in her body.'

'Speaking of romance, Meg, can I ring Mum and pretend I'm crashing here tonight? Please,' Kathy begged when Meg rolled her eyes. 'She's guarding me with her life.'

'She'll kill you if she finds out.'

Kathy laughed if she picked up the phone and dialled. 'No, she won't, Meg. She'll kill *you* for encouraging me.'

'That would be right,' Meg muttered taking the phone from a grinning Kathy. 'Yes, Mum, she is really here.' Taking an affectionate swipe at Kathy, she held the phone from her ear as Mary read the riot act.

'What did she say?' Kathy asked as Meg replaced the receiver.

'Plenty. ''You do realise you're not his bride until Saturday?'' ' She was mimicking her mother's voice. ' ''That you're wearing white for a reason and Jake might think less of you?'' '

'Bit late for that.' Kathy laughed, grabbing her bag and planting a quick kiss on her sister's cheek. 'Thanks so much, Meg.'

It was nice how they'd become close again, Meg reflected once Kathy had gone. Now that Meg had accepted Jake—accepted Kathy too, for that matter, as a woman not a little sister—their relationship had flourished. And, despite all the emotion over Flynn, and the pain she had been through, Meg really was looking forward to the wedding, to seeing her little sister say 'I do'.

Turning off the lights, Meg went to bed. Tonight she wasn't going to cry. Tonight she would think about Kathy, think about her dress and her shoes and all the pomp that came with a good old-fashioned wedding instead of dwelling on what might have been.

Her intentions were good, of course, but it was a red-eyed Meg who awoke the next morning. Yes, Meg decided, flicking on the kettle and shivering in her flimsy nightie, she might well be happy for Kathy, and, yes, she would enjoy the wedding. But other people's joy didn't soothe your own pain, only exacerbated your loss.

At least she didn't have to go to work today and smile politely at him. She was off now until after the wedding, and then all she had to do was serve her notice. So she filled her day buying all the things she would usually have organised ages ago—like stockings and a new eyeliner pen. Well, that was what she'd meant to buy, but, staggering back into the flat laden down with carrier bags, Meg decided that shopping really was the best cure for a broken heart—albeit a temporary one. But she'd take whatever she could get at the moment.

It was only when the clock edged to ten to six that Meg started to worry. Kathy had definitely said that she'd pick her up; Meg was sure of it. She had been ready for ages, changing her outfit umpteen times before putting back what she'd had on in the first place: a simple rust silk wraparound skirt with a small black top and some very new, very gorgeous Indian-looking sandals.

As was seemingly always the case, Kathy's mobile was turned off. In a spur-of-the-moment choice Meg decided she'd take Kathy's wrath any day of the week rather than her mother's if she was late, so scribbled an apologetic note telling Kathy she'd meet her at the church, pinned it to the door and clattered her way down the stairs in her new sandals—which were already starting to rub.

'Where have you been, Megan?' Mary demanded. One look at her sister's guilt-ridden face and Meg realised that Kathy had only now remembered that she was supposed to be picking her up

'Sorry, the traffic was terrible.'

'Which is why you should have left earlier. Now, come on, we've only got the church for half an hour.'

They might have only had the church for half an hour, but that didn't stop them from being put through their paces.

'You're supposed to be smiling as you walk up the aisle.'

'I will be, Mum, on Saturday.' Meg's sandals were really hurting now, and following a giggling Kathy for the tenth time really wasn't helping matters. Neither did the fact that Flynn, dressed in jeans and a T-shirt and looking absolutely delicious, was smothering a smile as Mary told her off.

'Okay, just one more time. Not you, Meg,' she barked. 'Just Kathy and Dad. I want to see them from

the church doors and check how they look from behind. Flynn, you stand next to Jake like the book
says.'

'She's not going to hum the "Bridal March" again,
is she?' Flynn asked as the trio disappeared, and even
Meg giggled.

But the smile soon vanished when Kathy came running through the church doors, an anguished look on
her face. 'Meg, you'd better come,' she said breathlessly. 'Mum's having palpitations.'

'I'll get my bag from the car,' Flynn said, moving
like lightning down the aisle. But Kathy put up her
hand to stop him. 'Not those sort, Flynn.' Her eyes
turned to Meg. 'Vince just turned up.'

'Vince!' Meg's shocked voice seemed amplified in
the hallowed silence of the church. 'But how did he
even know that I was here?'

'That was Mum's question, actually.' Kathy was
trying desperately to keep the mood light, but she
gave up when she realised no one else was even attempting a smile. 'He went to the flat and found your
note for me on the door. He wants to see you.'

'Well, I don't want to see him,' Meg said firmly.
'You can tell him that from me.'

Kathy shook her head. 'There's something else.
Apparently he's left his wife. Meg, I really think you
need to talk to him.'

'There's nothing left to say. Just get rid of him,
please, Kathy,' she urged.

'Your sister's got enough to contend with, without
doing your dirty work.' Mary marched towards them,
her face contorted with rage. *'Bloody Vince.'*

If it hadn't been such an awful moment Meg would have registered that it was the first time she had actually heard her mother swear. Mary clapped her hands over her mouth as soon as the mild expletive escaped her lips. 'Now look what you've made me do—and in God's house too. I mean it, Megan, go and sort things out once and for all.'

For a second she looked over to Flynn—hoping for what, she didn't know—but he looked as relaxed and carefree as ever, and Meg realised there and then that she was on her own. Vince was her problem and it was up to her deal with it.

'Meg,' Vince started as she marched angrily out of the church towards him, 'I'm sorry if I upset your mum.'

'No, you're not,' Meg retorted angrily. 'Just what on earth made you think you could come here?'

'I needed to see you…'

'Now?' Her voice was rising. 'You decide you need to see me and that's it? Doesn't it matter to you that I might be in the middle of something?' She gave a cynical snort before continuing. 'But then what does a wedding mean to you? Not much, obviously.'

'Meg, I've left Rhonda. My marriage is over.'

'So?' Meg shouted. 'Tell someone who cares.'

'Please, Meg.' He was pleading with her, and, looking up, she saw how tired and utterly awful he looked. 'Please. I just want five minutes. If you still don't want me then I'll walk away.'

'I don't want you, Vince.' Her voice was definite. 'Nothing you can say will change that.'

'Five minutes. Please,' he added desperately.

She didn't owe him anything, not a single thing, but maybe Meg was curious as to what he had to say, or hopeful that hearing him out might bring her some finality. They simply couldn't go on like this. With a small shrug she nodded.

'Can we go to your flat?'

'No. There's a café down the road; you can speak to me there.'

Meg declined his offer of something to eat, in fact she chose iced coffee in the hope that she could drink it quickly and get out of there.

'I'm sorry for lying to you,' Vince began. 'And if it's any consolation I really did love you. I just didn't want to hurt Rhonda.'

'You hurt us both.' The waitress brought over their drinks and Meg fiddled with the teaspoon, dunking it in and out of her drink—anything other than look at him.

'I know that,' Vince said sadly. 'When we broke up, I really tried hard to make my marriage work, but all I could think about was you. I've left her for you, Meg.'

'No, you haven't,' Meg said slowly. 'You've left Rhonda because your marriage wasn't working—it hasn't been since the day you asked me out, and probably not for a while before that.'

'But it's over now. Can't we try again? Wipe the slate clean? I know you don't trust me, but, given a chance, in time I could show you how I've changed—earn back your trust.'

Meg gave him an incredulous look. 'You shouldn't have to earn back my trust, Vince. You had it, every last piece of it, and you ripped it up and threw it away. It's gone. I don't know how to say it any clearer: I'm never going to trust you and I'm never going to love you.'

He sat there, staring into the disintegrating froth on his cappuccino, and with a start Meg realised his eyes were brimming with tears.

'So it's over?'

Hallelujah, Meg almost said, but stopped herself. His pain, his desolation, gave her no surge of triumph, no sense of vengeance. It was all just a sorry mess.

'It's over,' she said softly. Reaching across the table, she patted his arm. 'But you'll survive, and so will Rhonda. I'm living proof. Look, Vince, I really have to go. I'm in the middle of a wedding rehearsal.'

It was an utterly innocent gesture, a compassionate final touch before she got up and walked away, and had she glanced out of the window Meg would probably have thought twice about it. But she didn't look up. She didn't see Flynn standing on the pavement rummaging in his jeans for his car keys, or the pain in his eyes as he drove away.

'Can I call you?' Vince asked. 'Not yet—in a few weeks, maybe. We could try and be friends.'

Meg shook her head. 'No, Vince, we can never be friends. I mean that. I don't want you calling me, not ever.'

Placing some money on the table, she didn't even say goodbye, and she walked out of the café with her head held high, knowing in her heart that she'd done nothing wrong and wondering just why, then, did she feel so guilty?

CHAPTER TEN

MEG actually awoke not with a smile on her face, but for the first time in weeks with a sense of peace.

She was going to be all right.

Better than all right, she was going to be fine. Who needed a man? Okay, maybe years down the track it might possibly happen, but she wasn't going to die waiting. There was simply too much to do—the world was her oyster, so to speak. The surgical day ward would just have to wait. She had enough in the bank to take a dream cruise and banish all the horrible memories once and for all. And, Meg decided, lying staring at the ceiling, if she was going to be a spinster why not go the whole hog and get a cat?

But who would look after the cat when she went on her cruise?

There were a million and one things to be done today—from important things, like picking up various relatives from the airport or train station, right down to necessary basics, like washing her hair today so it wasn't too slippery when the hairdresser put it up, and tweezing her eyebrows to match the photo of Audrey Hepburn that Meg had faithfully cut out of a glossy magazine and stuck on the mantelpiece.

Meg was sleeping at the family home tonight—heaven only knew how, as practically every O'Sullivan in the phone book had been offered a bed for the night, much to Kathy's horror. Meg had been assigned a sleeping bag on the floor of her sister's room. And, despite the prospect of a hard floor and Kathy's grinding teeth, Meg was looking forward to it in a mawkish kind of way. Looking forward to sharing a room with her sister for probably the last time. No doubt in a couple of years when the families converged, Kathy's room would be overflowing with travel cots and squeaky toys. But not tonight. Tonight it was just the two of them.

Flynn.

He popped into her mind, as he always did, but Meg couldn't deal with it today—simply couldn't go there and be expected to keep on smiling. Throwing back the sheets, she forced his image from her mind, flicking on the coffee machine and darting down the communal stairs. Her neighbours bade her g'day with barely a glance; Meg in her heart-patterned pyjama shorts and skimpy crop top, rushing to collect her newspaper, was an all too familiar sight.

What wasn't a familiar sight, Meg realised, as she picked up the paper the newspaper boy had tossed onto the grass, was the huge silver car parked on the street. Correction, it *was* familiar—very familiar. And so was the six-foot, dark-haired, delicious package climbing out of it and walking towards her.

'We need to talk.'

Meg nodded dumbly, suddenly acutely aware of her lack of attire. 'How long have you been there?'

Flynn shrugged. 'All night. Is he still here?'

On closer inspection, Meg figured he was speaking the truth. Though still looking delicious, his T-shirt was crumpled like an old dishcloth and his chin certainly hadn't met a razor for a while. 'Who?'

'Who do you think?' He sounded irritated. 'Vince, of course.'

'Vince isn't here,' Meg said, confused. 'He never has been. Honestly,' she insisted when he gave her an unbelieving look. 'Why on earth would you be sitting outside?'

Flynn completely ignored her question; he obviously had other things on his mind. 'So what was that little tête-à-tête I saw you both engaging in?'

'Flynn, I've no idea what you're talking about.' For once it was Meg sounding rational, Meg who sounded in control. It was Flynn who was obviously struggling to hold it together. 'Look, do you want to come inside?'

He nodded and walking back to the flat, held the door open for her. Meg hesitated before going inside. Oh, she wasn't nervous of Flynn—not for a second—she was more worried about going first up the stairs in a skimpy pair of shorts, which seemed a stupid thing to be getting worked up about, given the turn of events.

But she found it easier to focus on trivialities, too scared to let her mind leap ahead and ask the bigger questions—scared, so scared, of building up her hopes only to have them cruelly dashed again.

'Do you want coffee?'

He shook his head impatiently. 'I didn't come for breakfast, Meg, I want to talk.'

'Fine,' Meg replied curtly, stalling for time, not sure whether or not she wanted to hear what he had to say to her. 'I'll have a coffee while you do the talking.' She held up the jug. 'Last chance.'

The aroma of the fresh brew got Flynn down from his moral high ground a touch, and grudgingly he nodded. An uncomfortable night in a parked car, however luxurious the model, wasn't the best prelude to what he had to say, and strong, sweet black coffee was just too tempting an offer to refuse.

She carried the drinks through to the lounge and sat down, determined not to let him see how flustered she was feeling, determined not to be the one to break the uncomfortable silence.

'He'll only hurt you,' Flynn blurted out. 'He might say he loves you, that he's left his wife, but he's cheated before and he'll do it again.'

Meg just sat there, sipping her coffee, refusing point-blank to look at him.

'And even if he doesn't cheat you're going to spend your life wondering. Every time he says he's going to be late, every time there's a wrong number on the telephone you'll work yourself up into a frenzy wondering if this is it.'

'And you sat outside all night to tell me this?'

'Yes,' Flynn said simply. 'After the church I went around to your parents'. They were all a bit upset. Your mum wanted to march around and talk some sense into you, but I said I'd do it. I've been up to your door countless times in the night—half of me wanted to break it down, to give Vince what he deserves, while the other half of me knew it would be pointless, that you have to make up your own mind, see what a loser he is for yourself.'

'But I have already. I did the day I found out he was married.' Her voice was starting to rise, a smouldering anger in her starting to ignite. 'For months now I've been telling everyone it's over—you, Mum, Kathy—yet none of you would listen. Why? Do you all think I'm so weak, so desperate that I'd take him back?'

'No.' He rose to his feet, running an exasperated hand through his hair before sitting back down again. 'No one thinks that, Meg.'

'Then why didn't anyone believe me when I said it was over?'

He stared at her for the longest time before answering. 'I guess we were all just scared.'

'Scared?' She gave a questioning, cynical laugh.

'Your mum and Kathy love you. I guess they were scared of seeing you get hurt.'

'And what about you, Flynn? Why were you scared?'

'Because I love you too.'

And though the words were sweet and beautiful Meg had heard them before.

Before he'd promptly turned around and broken her heart.

'You've already told me that, Flynn, but it didn't stop you ending it. It didn't stop you telling me that I was too suspicious and needy to merit you putting in what a relationship needs.'

'Yes,' he admitted. 'But, hell, Meg, I've never had a jealous bone in my body until now. Seeing you and Vince together, sitting in my car, thinking you were up here making love to him, I finally understood where you were coming from.'

She stared at him, unblinking. The fact that they loved each other wasn't in question here; it was how they dealt with their pasts that was tearing them apart.

'Not good enough, Flynn,' Meg finally answered, her voice unmoved. 'So you were jealous; so you finally got a taste of how I was feeling. Just what's that supposed to prove? Jealousy isn't our only problem, but you refuse to acknowledge that.'

'No, I don't.' His voice was a pale whisper. 'You were right. I'm not over Lucy. All that bull about celebrating her life, not mourning her death—all the big speeches about better to have loved and lost...' His voice trailed off and he cleared his throat before turning his eyes back to Meg. 'None of it was true, but I wasn't lying when I said it. I truly believed I was coping, that I was over her.'

Meg felt the tears well in her eyes—tears for his pain and tears for herself too. He wasn't over Lucy, she had known it in her heart, but hearing it confirmed, knowing he wasn't ready to move on, felt like the final twist of the knife.

'I'm so tired, Meg, so torn and tired. All I want to do, all I can do, is get away for a while. I rang Dr Campbell from the car this morning; he's going to give me some unpaid leave.' He gave a half-laugh but there was no humour in it. 'Somehow I doubt even he could get compassionate leave approved by Personnel two years after the event.'

'Well, they should. There's no blueprint.' Her voice was strangely high. 'People deal with these things in their own way. I know you need time, Flynn, but I don't know what you expect me to say here.' She swallowed nervously, scared of saying the wrong thing, scared of putting on too much pressure that might send him scuttling away. But if she couldn't be honest, couldn't even tell him this, then there wasn't much point.

No point at all.

'I'll wait for you.'

'Meg, you don't…' He took a step towards her but she put up her hand.

'Let me finish, Flynn.' Tears were pouring down her cheeks, but there was no hysteria in her voice, just calm tones mingled with a quiet dignity. 'I was mortified when I found out about Vince. Mortified that I could have been so fooled, so used, and mortified for what I'd done to his wife and my own family.'

'It wasn't your fault.'

'I know,' she admitted. 'But it was how I felt. And, rightly or wrongly, I was embarrassed, humiliated. But the tears I cried, the pain I felt, they weren't about Vince. Any love I had died there and then when I found out. Do you understand that?'

There was something in her voice that told him it was imperative he did, and he nodded.

'But when you and I broke up I was devastated. Not for anyone else, not over what people might think—I was devastated for us. For you and for me. And if you can understand that, then you'll know why I'm prepared to wait. Maybe you'll come back a different person—maybe I won't fit into your picture any more. And if that's the case then all you have to do is say so. I'll survive. I'll just carry right on. But if you do come back, and if you do still love me, then I'll be right here waiting.'

'Can I talk now?' Flynn's voice had all of its usual flip assurance, but the tears in his eyes told her he was moved. She sat down, the emotion of her speech having left her drained, almost numb. Nothing more could hurt her now.

'You don't have to wait for me, Meg. You don't have to wait for me because I'm not going anywhere without you.' He sat beside her and took her trembling hand as hope flickered on her face. 'I *can't* go anywhere without you. We've both been to hell and back, and we're both coming out of it, but we're coming out of it together. We're going to disappear for a month and lie on a beach in the day and hold each other at night. I want to grieve for Lucy, and I'm ready to do it now, but I want you beside me, Meg.' He took her in his arms then. 'I can't do this without you. Does that sound strange?'

She didn't answer with words. The tiny shake of her head against his chest told him she understood.

'When you were in my office, when you asked me why I came back to Emergency, it made me realise that I didn't even know what the hell I was doing there. What it was I was trying to prove.'

'You're not going to leave too?' She half-laughed, half-sobbed.

'No,' Flynn said slowly. 'Because even though it hurts like hell, even though it's sometimes the last place I want to be, it's still the best job in the world.

And I know that deep down in there...' He tapped gently at her chest as he kissed the top of her head. 'Deep down in there, you love it too. Don't hand in your notice, Meg,' he whispered. 'Not yet. You need a break, a rest, and then, if you're still feeling the same when we come back, go for it—move on without a backward glance. But don't throw your career away just yet. You're tired and you're burnt out, but you're still a wonderful nurse.'

'I don't really want to leave,' Meg admitted. 'But I can't go on doing it feeling like this.'

'Those days are gone now, Meg,' Flynn said, his voice trembling with emotion. 'You're never going to be crying in the car on your way home from work again because there'll be no need. You'll be coming home to me.'

She closed her eyes, revelling in the soft caress of his words, the glimpse of the future with Flynn beside her.

'We can't promise each other that we're going to make everything all right, can't promise that we're going to take away all the pain. But we can be there for each other, and surely that can only make things better?'

Her kiss was his answer, and hot salty tears were mingling, uniting, as they held each other close. 'I'd marry you tomorrow if it wouldn't steal Kathy's thunder.'

Meg laughed, but he noticed she was chewing her lip nervously.

'What? Come on, Meg, you can't not tell me.'

Meg pulled away. 'Flynn, about going on holiday… There's nothing I want more than to go away with you, but I don't think I can. I know you'll think I'm silly. It's just…'

'Just what?'

Meg swallowed. 'Mum would have a fit if I told her I was going on holiday with you—with any man, come to that.'

'But you're twenty-eight, for heaven's sake.' There was a humorous glint in his eye but Meg was too worked up to notice.

'I know, but it's just the way she is. I wouldn't expect you to understand. I just can't hurt her like that.'

'I think you underestimate your mum.'

'Believe me, I don't,' Meg muttered.

'Oh, yes, you do.' He popped a kiss on her nose. 'I've already asked her, and she's fine with it.'

Meg's jaw dropped to the floor. 'You never did?'

'I did.' Flynn grinned, then winced dramatically. 'A slight exaggeration—she wasn't exactly fine, but she soon came around.'

'How?'

'Are you busy today?'

'Impossibly,' Meg said, bemused. 'I've got to pick up Aunt Morag, my cousins, do some shopping…' she glanced up at Audrey, smiling demurely from the mantelpiece '…pluck my eyebrows.'

'Well, add ''Buy an engagement ring'' to your list,' Flynn said blithely, but there was a small muscle flickering in his cheek. 'Because if there's not a ring on your finger by the wedding tomorrow then the deal's off. According to your mother it had better be a ring that can be seen from the back rows of the church.'

'She never said that.' Meg laughed.

'And plenty more besides.' Taking her hands, he stood her up. 'Come on, we'd better get a move on.'

Though Meg couldn't wipe the smile off her face, she wondered how Flynn could even think about shopping at a time like this! 'I'd better get dressed first.'

His fingers were toying with her crop top. 'You'd better, hadn't you?' He gave a dramatic sigh. 'And if we're going to have any hope of getting things done today I guess I'll just have to give you a hand.'

Aunt Morag, her hair, her eyebrows—they didn't even merit a thought as he slithered the top over Meg's head.

Flynn was beside her now.

They'd get there in the end.

MILLS & BOON®

JANUARY 2003 HARDBACK TITLES

ROMANCE™

The Blind-Date Bride *Emma Darcy*	H5732	0 263 17579 0
Keir O'Connell's Mistress *Sandra Marton*	H5733	0 263 17580 4
Back in the Boss's Bed *Sharon Kendrick*	H5734	0 263 17581 2
The Spaniard's Woman *Diana Hamilton*	H5735	0 263 17582 0
Passion in Secret *Catherine Spencer*	H5736	0 263 17583 9
Husband by Arrangement *Sara Wood*	H5737	0 263 17584 7
Claiming His Bride *Daphne Clair*	H5738	0 263 17585 5
Wed by a Will *Cara Colter*	H5739	0 263 17586 3
An Accidental Engagement *Jessica Steele*	H5740	0 263 17587 1
The Marriage Market *Leigh Michaels*	H5741	0 263 17588 X
Almost Married *Darcy Maguire*	H5742	0 263 17589 8
The Tycoon Prince *Barbara McMahon*	H5743	0 263 17590 1
Finding Her Prince *Lilian Darcy*	H5744	0 263 17591 X
Daddy's Double Due Date *Belinda Barnes*	H5745	0 263 17592 8
Emergency at Bayside *Carol Marinelli*	H5746	0 263 17593 6
Dating Dr Carter *Judy Campbell*	H5747	0 263 17594 4

HISTORICAL ROMANCE™

The Chaperon Bride *Nicola Cornick*	H543	0 263 17819 6
The Decadent Countess *Deborah Miles*	H544	0 263 17820 X

MEDICAL ROMANCE™

The Doctor's Destiny *Meredith Webber*	M461	0 263 17843 9
The Surgeon's Proposal *Lilian Darcy*	M462	0 263 17844 7

1202 Gen Std HB

MILLS & BOON®

JANUARY 2003 LARGE PRINT TITLES

ROMANCE™

A Passionate Surrender *Helen Bianchin*	1543	0 263 17867 6
The Heiress Bride *Lynne Graham*	1544	0 263 17868 4
His Virgin Mistress *Anne Mather*	1545	0 263 17869 2
To Marry McAllister *Carole Mortimer*	1546	0 263 17870 6
Mistaken Mistress *Margaret Way*	1547	0 263 17871 4
The Bedroom Assignment *Sophie Weston*	1548	0 263 17872 2
The Pregnancy Bond *Lucy Gordon*	1549	0 263 17873 0
A Royal Proposition *Marion Lennox*	1550	0 263 17874 9

HISTORICAL ROMANCE™

The Rebellious Débutante *Meg Alexander*	241	0 263 17987 7
The Knight's Conquest *Juliet Landon*	242	0 263 17988 5

MEDICAL ROMANCE™

Emergency Groom *Josie Metcalfe*	445	0 263 17963 X
His Brother's Son *Jennifer Taylor*	446	0 263 17964 8
The Doctor's Mistress *Lilian Darcy*	447	0 263 17965 6
Dr Preston's Daughter *Laura MacDonald*	448	0 263 17966 4

1202 Gen Std LP

MILLS & BOON®

FEBRUARY 2003 HARDBACK TITLES

ROMANCE™

The Pregnancy Proposal *Helen Bianchin*	H5748	0 263 17595 2
Alejandro's Revenge *Anne Mather*	H5749	0 263 17596 0
Marco's Pride *Jane Porter*	H5750	0 263 17645 2
City Cinderella *Catherine George*	H5751	0 263 17646 0
A Sicilian Husband *Kate Walker*	H5752	0 263 17647 9
Blackmailed by the Boss *Kathryn Ross*	H5753	0 263 17648 7
At the Millionaire's Bidding *Lee Wilkinson*	H5754	0 263 17649 5
A Spanish Inheritance *Susan Stephens*	H5755	0 263 17650 9
Rush to the Altar *Rebecca Winters*	H5756	0 263 17651 7
The Venetian Playboy's Bride *Lucy Gordon*	H5757	0 263 17652 5
Her Secret Millionaire *Jodi Dawson*	H5758	0 263 17653 3
A Wedding at Windaroo *Barbara Hannay*	H5759	0 263 17654 1
Traveling Man *Leigh Michaels*	H5760	0 263 17655 X
The Heiress Bride *Laurey Bright*	H5761	0 263 17656 8
Delivering Secrets *Fiona McArthur*	H5762	0 263 17657 6
His Emergency Fiancée *Kate Hardy*	H5763	0 263 17658 4

HISTORICAL ROMANCE™

An Unconventional Heiress *Paula Marshall*	H545	0 263 17821 8
Kitty *Elizabeth Bailey*	H546	0 263 17822 6

MEDICAL ROMANCE™

Daisy and the Doctor *Meredith Webber*	M463	0 263 17845 5
The Surgeon's Marriage *Maggie Kingsley*	M464	0 263 17846 3

MILLS & BOON®

FEBRUARY 2003 LARGE PRINT TITLES

ROMANCE™

The Contaxis Baby *Lynne Graham*	1551	0 263 17875 7
Marco's Convenient Wife *Penny Jordan*	1552	0 263 17876 5
Sarah's Secret *Catherine George*	1553	0 263 17877 3
The Italian's Demand *Sara Wood*	1554	0 263 17878 1
A Professional Marriage *Jessica Steele*	1555	0 263 17879 X
The Baby Bombshell *Day Leclaire*	1556	0 263 17880 3
Accidental Bride *Darcy Maguire*	1557	0 263 17881 1
The Sheikh's Proposal *Barbara McMahon*	1558	0 263 17882 X

HISTORICAL ROMANCE™

Jack Compton's Luck *Paula Marshall*	243	0 263 17989 3
The Duke's Mistress *Ann Elizabeth Cree*	244	0 263 17990 7

MEDICAL ROMANCE™

Accidental Seduction *Caroline Anderson*	449	0 263 17967 2
The Spanish Doctor *Margaret Barker*	450	0 263 17968 0
The ER Affair *Leah Martyn*	451	0 263 17969 9
Emergency: Doctor in Need *Lucy Clark*	452	0 263 17970 2

0103 Gen Std LP